just in case

Also by Meg Rosoff

How I Live Now

meg rosoff

just in case

WENDY
LAMB
BOOKS

Special thanks to Liz Elowe for advice and support

Published by Wendy Lamb Books
an imprint of Random House Children's Books
a division of Random House, Inc.
New York

www.randomhouse.com/teens

Educators and librarians, for a variety of teaching tools, visit us at
www.randomhouse.com/teachers

Library of Congress Cataloging-in-Publication Data

Rosoff, Meg.
Just in case / Meg Rosoff.
p. cm.
Summary: Convinced that fate is out to get him, fifteen-year-old David Case assumes a new identity in the hope of avoiding what he believes is certain doom.
ISBN-13: 978-0-385-74678-6 (trade) — ISBN-13: 978-0-385-90909-9 (lib. bdg.)
ISBN-10: 0-385-74678-4 (trade) — ISBN-10: 0-385-90909-8 (lib. bdg.)
[1. Fate and fatalism—Fiction. 2. Brothers—Fiction. 3. England—Fiction.] I. Title.
PZ7.R71957Jus 2006
[Fic]—dc22

2006002023

Printed in the United States of America

10 9 8 7 6 5 4 3 2 1

First Edition

For Paul

just in case

The view is fine up here. I can look out across the world and see everything.

For instance, I can see a fifteen-year-old boy and his brother.

1

DAVID CASE'S BABY BROTHER had recently learned to walk but he wasn't what you'd call an expert. He toddled past his brother to the large open window of the older boy's room. There, with a great deal of effort, he pulled himself onto the windowsill, scrunched up like a caterpillar, pushed into a crouch, and stood, teetering precariously, his gaze fixed solemnly on the church tower a quarter mile away.

He tipped forward slightly towards the void just as a large black bird swooped past. It paused and turned an intelligent red eye to meet the child's.

"Why not fly?" suggested the bird, and the boy's eyes widened in delight.

Below them on the street, a greyhound stood motionless,

his elegant pale head turned in the direction of the incipient catastrophe. Calmly the dog shifted the angle of his muzzle, creating an invisible guyline that eased the child back an inch or two towards equilibrium. Safer now, but seduced by the fact that a bird had spoken to him, the boy threw out his arms and thought, Yes! Fly!

David did not hear his brother think "fly."

Something else made him look up. A voice. A finger on his shoulder. The brush of lips against his ear.

So that's where we start: One boy on the verge of death. Another on the verge of something rather more complicated.

In the instant of looking up, David took the measure of the situation, shouted "*Charlie!*" and lunged across the room. He grabbed the child by the cape of his Batman pajamas, wrapped his arms around him with enough force to flatten his ribs, and sank to the floor, squashing the boy's face into the safe hollow beneath his chin.

Charlie squeaked with outrage but David barely heard. Panting, he unpinned him, gripping the child at arm's length.

"What were you doing?" He was shouting. "What on earth did you think you were doing?"

Well, said Charlie, I was bored just playing with my toys and you weren't paying attention to me so I thought I would get a better look at the world. I climbed up on the window which wasn't easy and once I managed to do that I felt strange and happy with nothing but sky all around me and all of a sudden a bird flew past and looked at me and said I could fly and a bird hasn't ever talked to me before and I figured a bird would know what he was talking about when it came to flying so I thought he must be right. Oh and there was also a pretty gray dog on the pavement who looked up and pointed at me with his nose so I didn't fall and just when I was about to leap out and soar through the air you grabbed me and hurt me a lot which made me very cross and I didn't get a chance to fly even though I'm sure I could have.

The little boy explained all this slowly and carefully, so as not to be misunderstood.

"Burr-dee fly" were the words that came out of his mouth.

David turned away, heart pounding. It was useless trying to communicate with a one-year-old. Even if his brother had possessed the vocabulary, he couldn't have answered David's question. Charlie did what he did because he was a dumb kid, too dumb to realize that birds don't talk and kids can't fly.

My god, David thought. If I'd been two seconds slower he'd be dead. My brother would be dead but *I'd* be the one shattered, crushed, destroyed by guilt and blame and everyone everywhere for the rest of my life whispering *He's that kid who killed his brother*.

Two seconds. Just two seconds were all that stood between normal everyday life and utter, total catastrophe.

David sat down hard, head spinning. Why had this never occurred to him? He could fall down a manhole, collapse of a stroke. A car crash could sever his spinal cord. He could catch bird flu. A tree could fall on him. There were comets. Killer bees. Foreign armies. Floods. Serial killers. There was buried nuclear waste. Ethnic cleansing. Alien invasion.

A plane crash.

Suddenly, everywhere he looked he saw catastrophe, bloodshed, the demise of the planet, the ruin of the human race, not to mention (to pinpoint the exact source of his anxiety) possible pain and suffering to himself.

Who could have thought up a scenario this bleak?

Whoever (whatever) it was, he could feel the dark malevolence of it settling in, making itself at home like some vicious bird of prey, its sharp claws sunk deep into the quivering gray jelly of his terrified brain. He pulled his brother close, tucking him in against his body, pressed his lips to the child's face.

What if . . . ?

He became enmired in what if.

The weight of it wrapped itself around his ankles and dragged him under.

A YEAR EARLIER, David's father had woken him with a shout.

"David, your mother's home! Aren't you interested in seeing the baby?"

Not really, David thought, burying his head in his pillow. I know what a baby looks like.

But then they were in his room, grinning and making inane noises in the direction of a small, serene-looking creature with jet black eyes.

David sat up with a groan and peered at his new brother. OK, seen him, he thought.

"Of course he can't see *you* yet." His father, superior as ever. "Babies can't focus properly for weeks."

David was about to go back to sleep when he noticed the

new baby gazing at him with a peculiar expression of calm authority.

I'm Charlie, said the new baby's eyes, as clearly as if he had spoken the words out loud. Who are you?

David stared.

His brother repeated the question slowly, politely, as if to a person of limited intelligence. Who, exactly, are you?

David frowned.

The baby inclined his head, his face registering something that might have been pity. Such a simple question, he thought.

But if his brother knew the answer, he gave no sign.

This disturbed Charlie. Over the next few months, he tried approaching his parents for answers, but his father was always at work and his mother seemed strangely ill informed on the subject of her older son.

"He's usually on time," she would comment brightly, or "I wish he'd tidy his room more." But nothing about *who he was*. And when she caught Charlie staring intently at David, she merely thought, How sweet. They're bonding.

But they weren't bonding. Charlie was comparing the David he knew with the Davids he saw displayed around the house in family pictures. The younger Davids looked cheerful and carefree; they held books or bikes or ice creams and gazed at the camera with expressions of trust. The younger Davids kicked balls, swung from trees, blew out the candles on birthday cakes. They had clear edges and cloudless eyes.

But the David that Charlie knew now was wavery and fizzy with nerves. The new David reminded Charlie of a birthday card he'd seen where the picture of a clown shifted gradually into the picture of a tightrope walker, depending on how you tilted it. Exactly when this transformation had begun, the child couldn't say. According to the photos, his brother's outline had begun to blur sometime between playing football at thirteen and losing his status as only child the following year.

Charlie had spent a good deal of his short life worrying about his older brother. Now he paused in the middle of playing Monkey Rides in a Car with Donkey to gather his thoughts. He saw that his recent attempt to fly had been a mistake. It seemed to have nudged his brother past some invisible tipping point and this filled him with remorse. Charlie wanted to make amends, to offer advice on how David could regain his footing. But he couldn't get his brother to listen.

Or perhaps he *was* listening, but somehow lacked the capacity to understand. This worried Charlie most of all.

3

SOMEONE OTHER than David Case might have experienced the near catastrophe of that summer day and imagined he'd had a lucky escape.

Someone else in the dull suburban town of Luton might have thought that such things happen; taken it as a warning that all humans are fallible, that a certain degree of vigilance is required to avoid life's many potential tragedies.

Someone else might even have congratulated himself on saving his brother's life.

But David Case was not someone else. Months of half-formed worries and loosely framed paranoid fantasies clicked into place that afternoon with the finality of a proclamation. In a single instant, the vague confusion of images in his head resolved into certainty. He was doomed.

He lay in bed the following morning, replaying the scene in his head. He'd avoided tragedy this time, yes, but next time the arrow (the bullet, the boulder, the bomb) would find its mark. He could see the horrible scenario spooling out with the deceptive simplicity of a cartoon: fate wandering idly past, checking his watch, feigning indifference—and then *WHAMMO!*

Pulling on his clothes, he felt eyes watching him.

Pouring breakfast cereal into a bowl, he saw his life crashing down in smoking ruins.

Oh god, he thought, brushing his teeth. I have to hide. No, not hide. Mutate. Become unrecognizable.

He sat on his bed, bit his nails, took inventory. Fifteen years old, five foot nine inches tall, sloping shoulders, shuffling gait, reasonably polite, crooked teeth, medium-brown English hair, medium-fair English complexion.

None of these qualities would protect him from disaster. His only chance was to remake his life one step at a time, starting with his name. And if he managed to be different enough, well, perhaps fate would forget about David Case and pass on to the next pathetic victim. Hound *him* to death.

He stepped out his front door and off the curb, causing a cyclist to swerve in front of a delivery van, and changed his name to Justin. Justin sounded suave, coolly ironic, hard-bodied, rigorously intelligent. More competent than David. Less vulnerable. Justin Case was the sort of character who could cope with danger.

The screech and the sound of the impact stopped him momentarily and he watched with interest as the cyclist flew off his bike and into the air.

No matter what happened, Justin would be fluid, clever, and responsive. He would duck and dive, beat the odds. The cyclist crashed onto the roof of the van, bounced once off the windscreen, slid to the ground, and lay still.

Justin Case would not be listed in the social service records, on the county birth lists, in the plans for the future of mankind. David's heart soared. He could hear the approaching sound of ambulance and police sirens and continued on his way, not wanting to be the sort of person who stops to stare at other people's misfortunes.

As he rounded the corner he felt triumphant.

Nothing bad could happen to Justin Case because he did not exist.

4

JUSTIN (FORMERLY DAVID) had work to do. He had to change how he looked, exchange David's baggy jeans and sweatshirts, his sneakers and T-shirts, his unexceptional socks and mediocre anorak for the sort of clothes Justin Case might wear. In four months he would turn sixteen. He had always imagined everything would change when he turned sixteen, so why not start now?

He headed for the front door and found Charlie in the hall, balancing a small plastic hippo on the edge of a porcelain umbrella stand. Charlie looked up at his brother, startled, and dropped the animal into the abyss.

"Never mind." Justin reached into the deep cylinder and felt around for the toy, bringing it up with a handful of others.

"There's your hippo," he said, placing it in his brother's outstretched hand. "And a zebra, lion, goat, giraffe, cow. Why don't you play somewhere else? There's a whole lost animal kingdom down there."

I'm not playing, Charlie said, dropping them back down the umbrella stand one by one. I'm thinking about falling.

Justin shook his head. Young children seemed unable to grasp the simplest principles. "Suit yourself," he said, ruffling the child's hair. He went out the door and set off down the road.

For the practicalities of his transformation he had chosen a nearby charity shop. Inside were thousands of castoffs from other lives; surely one of them would fit him.

He walked the short distance to the shop feeling guilty and somewhat suspect, like a spy. The feeling was good. He had a mission.

Inside he hesitated, running his eyes over the racks of dowdy blouses, last decade's dresses, and scuffed shoes. The woman at the till, pinch-faced and scowling, glared at him but said nothing. In her eyes, he was obviously a shiftless, thieving young person with nothing better to do with the last days of his summer holiday than defraud charity shops of their chipped and valueless merchandise.

He stared back at her, eyes hard and emptied of emotion. The name was Case. Justin Case. If he wanted to try on a shirt, he would try on a shirt.

In the far corner, he spied a rack of men's clothing, crossed the floor to it, and pulled out a shirt. He held it up under his chin. It smelled of something, something not entirely pleasant.

Stale cigarettes, burnt potatoes, coconut soap. The thought of adopting another person's smell hadn't occurred to him, made him faintly queasy. He closed his eyes, trying to expel the image from his brain.

A voice at his elbow nearly caused him to jump out of his skin.

"Try this," the voice said. Its arm held out a dark brown and lavender paisley shirt.

Justin turned slowly. The voice belonged to a girl of perhaps nineteen who peered at him through a heavy, clipped pink fringe. Her eyes were thickly rimmed with kohl, her mouth neatly outlined in a vivid shade of orange that clashed perfectly with her hair. She wore four-inch platform boots in pale green snakeskin, wildly patterned tights, a very short skirt, and a tight see-through shirt printed with Japanese cartoons over which was squeezed a 1950s-style long-line beige elastic bra. A camera bag hung from her shoulder.

Even Justin recognized that her dress sense was unusual.

"Wow," he said.

"Thank you," she replied demurely. And then, "I've never seen you before." She tilted her head to one side, taking in his pale skin, lank hair, and good cheekbones. The dark circles under his eyes.

Doomed youth, she thought. Interesting.

Justin looked alarmed. "What?"

"I was just thinking. You could find some excellent things here if you knew what to look for."

"I know what I need."

She waited.

"Everything," he said at last. "Everything different in every way from this." He indicated himself.

"Everything?"

"Yes. I need a whole new identity."

She smiled. "Have you killed someone?"

He met her eyes. "Not yet."

The perfectly drawn orange mouth formed a tiny "*o*."

Justin turned away. When he looked back, she was still staring at him.

"You're a *potential* killer?"

He sighed. "A potential kill-ee, more like."

Her eyes narrowed. "Are you involved with drugs?"

"No."

"Blackmail?"

"No."

"Witness protection?"

"No."

"Spooks?"

He shook his head. "No, nothing like that."

"Then what?"

Justin fidgeted, shifting his weight from one foot to the other. He chewed his thumb. "I discovered my old self was doomed."

"Doomed?"

"Doomed."

"In what sense, doomed?"

"In the sense of standing poised on the brink of ruin with time running out."

She stared.

"Which is why I need to change everything. All of me. I can't be recognized."

The girl frowned. "But who do you think will recognize you?"

He dropped his voice. "Fate. My fate. David Case's fate."

"Who's David Case?"

"Me. That is, I used to be him. Before I started changing everything."

"You've changed your name?"

He nodded.

"So, you're running away from fate," the girl said slowly, "and you think all this is going to make a difference?"

He shrugged. "What else can I do?"

"Stop believing in fate?"

Justin sighed. "I wish I could."

Neither of them said anything for a long time. The girl studied a chip on one of her nails.

"Well," she said finally, with the smallest hint of a smile. "It's *different*."

He looked at her.

"Not uninteresting," she added.

"Not?"

"No." She raised an eyebrow. "*Not*."

She extended her hand. "My name is Agnes." The fingers she offered had pale green fingernails. "Agnes Bee."

"Justin. Justin Case."

She blinked, digesting this information. And then all at once she beamed, her face illuminated with delight. He took the hand she offered. It was surprisingly soft and warm, and he held it cautiously, not sure when to let go. He had no experience touching older women.

"How very nice to meet you, Justin Case." Still smiling, Agnes turned to one of the racks and pulled out a shirt: poppy colored, long sleeves, ruffle down the front. She thrust it at Justin, along with the brown and lavender paisley. "Try these. I'll keep looking."

Justin looked at the shirts. "I don't think so."

She ignored him.

He sighed, took the hangers, and entered the tiny changing room at the far end of the shop. There was barely room to turn sideways.

The first shirt fit. He buttoned it and looked around for a mirror.

Agnes swept the curtain aside and Justin found himself viewed in reverse close-up portrait through the wrong end of a Nikon 55mm DX lens. Click click click, click click click. Three frames per second. Two seconds. He leapt back with a startled squeak.

Agnes's face emerged from one side of her Nikon. "What?"

"What do you mean 'what?' *That*."

She frowned. "Turn around and let me look at you."

He turned around and let her look at him.

"Not bad." She beamed approval, then put down the camera and picked up a small pile of clothes. "I've been keeping an eye on these things for ages. For *exactly* the right person."

The thought of being exactly the right person appealed to Justin so completely that he tried everything she brought him and attempted to like it all. She brought him a turquoise flowered shirt, a skinny brown cardigan that he thought must have been designed for a woman, and a pair of white canvas trousers that had to be cinched with a belt. He put them all on and emerged from the cubicle, nervous.

Click click, click click click. Five shots aimed with deadly accuracy at his head. Agnes lowered her camera and considered him.

"Excellent. You'll take them all." She squinted, head turned slightly to one side. "You're very lucky I was here today."

Justin nodded uncertainly.

"Of course this is only the beginning." She spotted a red and white vinyl bowling bag and crossed briskly to pick it up.

Justin watched her. He had no idea what she was talking about, but the feeling fit with his new life as a stranger. There was even something reassuring about it.

Agnes carried the clothes to the till, accepted a small pile of creased five-pound notes from Justin, and handed them to the sour-faced woman. The money looked as if it had been crammed in a piggy bank for years, which it had.

"That's all he has," she told the scowling troll. "It'll have to do."

While the woman harrumphed and muttered irritably, Agnes flicked through her camera's digital display.

She looked up and gazed solemnly at Justin. "You photograph like an angel, Justin Case."

Was he being solicited for a child pornography Web site, or perhaps a fanzine article on fashion disasters?

"Never mind. Next time I'll bring proofs."

Next time?

"I've enjoyed our first meeting immensely."

He tried to smile, but it came out lopsided, uncertain. Click click click.

On the way out of the shop, Agnes spied a pair of pristine black jeans half hidden under a pile of shirts. She stopped short, examined them, and tossed them to Justin.

"Try them on."

She waited outside the tiny changing room as he pulled them on. They fit perfectly.

Agnes Bee swept back the curtain once more. "Could you scream?" she asked happily.

Justin nodded. He thought he probably could.

5

ALLOW ME to introduce myself.

My name is Kismet. Turkish, from Persian *qismat,* from Arabic *qisma,* lot, from *qasama,* to divide, allot. SYN: Chance. Providence. Destiny. Luck.

Fate.

I'm the one with my finger on the scale, the bullet, the brakes. The one who chooses which sperm, which egg, who lives, who dies.

Fate giveth, fate taketh away.

But we were talking about David.

Poor feckless little David, holding fast to his stunted little life. It could almost be amusing.

Almost.

You. Come closer. Let me whisper in your ear.

Your friend, your character, your *David* is a fool. A chump. A little white mouse with a pink twitching nose.

I have my paw on his tail.

Watch what happens when I lift it.

See? Let him have his little scamper.

I'm not hungry just now.

A little later, perhaps.

You'll know.

6

JUSTIN'S PARENTS REFUSED to address him by his new name.

"How do you expect us to change what we call you after all these years? It's unnatural."

He didn't even try explaining about his fate. He knew they weren't paying attention, what with all the first-time walking, talking, and weeing going on in other parts of the house.

Justin felt sure that unless they actually found him with a loaded gun in one hand and a suicide note in the other, they wouldn't worry overmuch about the levels and sources of his anxiety. But that was OK. He didn't expect much from his parents. He knew they were busy. He knew they'd tried to be good parents. They'd paid attention to him when he was younger, taken him to zoos and sports days, bought him snacks. Pretended his Christmas list really went to Santa. Gave him an instructional video about sex.

He also recognized that his younger brother was cuter, more biddable, and less philosophically challenging. Under the circumstances, his parents' preference for the baby made sense, as did their lack of understanding on the subject of their older son's doom. He didn't exactly understand it himself.

They had refrained from commenting on his recent metamorphosis, having read in the Sunday papers that teenagers were likely to behave in an eccentric manner, but Justin noticed his mother attempting to peer into his mouth sometimes when he spoke. He suspected she was looking for a tongue stud. The thought of such a piercing sickened him. It made him sad that this was the level on which she believed he operated.

"Hello, David," she said as usual on the morning he came down to breakfast in a poppy-colored shirt with a ruffle down the front and a pair of white trousers cinched with a belt.

She glanced at her husband, and a look passed between them suggesting a subject of previous and mutual concern. Folding his newspaper, Justin's father cleared his throat.

"David," he began in the manner of a pronouncement.

Justin raised his spoon to his mouth and paused.

"David. I want to know, that is, *we* want to know, to inquire really, your mother and I, neither here nor there in any real sense, simply to access the facts, well, ahem. That is to say. You're not homosexual, are you?"

Justin placed the spoon in his mouth and then returned it

slowly to the bowl. Across the table, his brother sucked on an apricot.

"No no no!" The little boy laughed, waving his arms emphatically to no one in particular.

"Because if you are, your mother and I want you to know it's fine."

Justin chewed and swallowed.

His parents glanced at each other.

"Well?" asked his mother anxiously.

Justin looked up, as if seeing her for the first time. "Yes?"

"Are you . . . ?" She blushed. "You know."

"HO-MO-SEX-UAL." Exasperation caused his father to shout.

Justin lifted his spoon and pondered the question. Milk dripped off it as it hovered, loaded, in midair. Homosexual? It hadn't really occurred to him. He supposed it was possible. Anything was possible.

"Not that I know of," he said finally.

His father exhaled impatiently and returned to his paper. "Well, that's a relief," he snorted. "Life's complicated enough without having a poof for a son."

7

SCHOOL STARTED the following Tuesday.

The radio blasted Justin awake at precisely 7:00 a.m. and he sat bolt upright in bed, shocked, blood pumping rapidly through alarmed organs. He hadn't been up before noon all summer.

Groaning, he flailed at the snooze button until the noise stopped, and fell once more into a deep sleep. At the fourth repeat, he sat up in bed, reached over, and pulled back one of the curtains.

It was pissing with rain.

The gloom was so thick he could barely see the road from the front window of his bedroom. He sighed, facing the prospect of a new school year with all the pleasure of a worm facing a beak.

I wish I had a dog, he thought, searching under the bed for his new paisley shirt and white canvas trousers.

Justin stood up and stopped with one arm in an armhole and one lying slack by his side. He felt suddenly that if he could walk into school today with a new name, new clothes, and a dog, the sleekest, most elegant greyhound in creation, he might possibly survive. But he had no greyhound, and the chances of getting hold of one before eight-thirty seemed tragically slim. It was already ten past.

He said goodbye to his mother, picked Charlie up off the floor, and whirled him around till he squeaked with glee. Then he shook hands with his father and set off to meet his fate.

The thought of a pet, even an imaginary pet, soothed him. He stopped in the drizzle along the half-mile walk to school so that his dog could sniff lampposts, trees, dead birds.

Here, boy! Come on, boy!

He called his greyhound happily. The creature possessed an effortless grace combined with serenity, dignity, wisdom. The dog's soft eyes contemplated the world with calm compassion. His body was smooth and elegant, his chest deep, legs strong and well defined. What a combination of the physical and the spiritual! Surely no ordinary dog, no mere mortal dog could claim the attributes of—of—of Boy.

Good Boy! Boy was no poodle. Anyone could see that.

As he reached the school gates, Justin found himself in the midst of an excited crowd of hormonally charged human particles, each one bouncing randomly off its fellow particles, converging finally into groups of twos and threes. Each group pursued the age-old business of swapping cigarette ends and lies about summer sexual conquests, picking up old friendships and resuming grudges exactly where they left off.

The new term held endless golden promise: new victims for bullies, new excuses to fail literacy and play truant, new opportunities to pursue what their parents laughably referred to as an education.

"Hey, Case!" He heard a wolf whistle. "Nice shirt."

It was an education all right.

Justin nodded, exchanging greetings with a variety of individuals, many of whom he had known since primary school. Some could be categorized as friends, some were nodding acquaintances. Most knew his name.

It was not going to be easy to explain his new identity.

He turned to Boy, and the greyhound slipped his velvety muzzle into Justin's hand. He left it there for a long moment, imparting strength, grace, and wisdom to his owner. Justin felt himself illuminated by the contact, fortified by the touch of his fabulous beast.

"*Hola*."

He looked up. Peter Prince was fair-haired, toweringly tall and skinny, with bony knees and a relentlessly cheerful smile. He was known (if at all) for his peculiar genius in matters relating to astronomy. He and Justin crossed paths only in Spanish and history, subjects at which neither excelled.

"Good summer?"

"Only if you like psychic torment," Justin said.

"That's too bad." Peter appeared genuinely sympathetic. "I don't suppose today's going to be much of an improvement."

"No."

Peter looked at him closely. There was definitely something different about David Case. It wasn't just his clothes, though they certainly suggested a calamity of some sort. It was an air of unease. Bordering on crisis. Not that David had ever been convincingly average, Peter thought, though perhaps he'd managed to convince himself. People did.

Peter frowned, struggling to piece together the puzzle, but before he could reach a conclusion the bell rang and they were swept through into the Victorian building's main hall on a scrambling tide of humanity.

Justin found a seat in his first class with Peter to his left and Boy sprawled at his feet.

"Welcome back, et cetera, et cetera, et cetera," intoned Mr. Ogle, with the jaded air of a factory pieceworker at the end of a forty-eight-hour shift. Eleven seconds into the new school year and already he radiated weariness. "You are no doubt as happy to be here as I am. I can only hope"—he scanned the thirty faces in the room, some innocent, some insolent, the rest mainly blank with indifference—"that this year will be less of a trial than last."

The class shuffled with doubt.

Mr. Ogle pulled out the class register.

Justin's heart began to pound. Oh god, he thought. Here we go.

"Archer, James."

"Yeah."

"Bodmin, Amanda."

"Yah."

"Cadaprakash, Matthew."

"Yes."

"Case, David."

Justin raised his hand halfway. "Justin, actually."

Mr. Ogle stopped and looked at the register. "David, surely? *David* Case, unless I'm grossly mistaken?"

Justin shook his head. "No. It's Justin."

"Justin Case? *Just-in-Case?*"

He looked up at the class, his features uncharacteristically animated. "Is this some sort of joke?"

The class evidently thought it was. It was bad enough that David Case had arrived for school so peculiarly dressed. But to have changed his name as well? The first-day tensions dissolved into timid chuckles which spread clockwise around the room, gaining momentum until Justin's fellow students were choking, then screaming with laughter, tears rolling down their faces.

Peter looked down at his hands, embarrassed for the student formerly known as David.

Mr. Ogle whacked his book against the wall with a resounding *crack!* and his delirious charges fell silent. The silence had an exhausted, joyous quality and Justin slumped in his chair, hoping to remain invisible in the aftermath. But the forty minutes that followed caused his hope to evaporate in a flurry of sideways glances, sniggers, and whispers. The moment class finished, he stood up, arranged his features into a blank, looked neither left nor right, moved at a steady pace. He knew better than to thrash about. As long as there was no trace of blood in the water he'd be safe.

Not that it mattered, he told himself. He had bigger fish to fry. Bigger fish had him to fry.

With a sympathetic smile and a wave, Peter left for his next class while Justin steeled himself for a day of humiliation. His few tenuous allies dwindled in number as the day went on. The joke played to responsive audiences in six more subjects.

At precisely three-thirty, the bell rang and he went home, slammed the front door, and collapsed in a chair. His mother looked up from folding laundry and smiled.

"How was school, darling?"

"Hell."

"What about your classes?"

"Torture."

"And your friends?"

"Scum."

His mother considered him, frowning. "You're not in trouble of any sort, are you, David?" She pondered the matter, her brow furrowed. If he wasn't homosexual, perhaps he was dyslexic? The tabloids often cited dyslexia (school lunches, overcrowding, immigration, absent fathers) as a source of problems at school.

"David, love, tell me. Can you tell the difference between 'dog' and 'god'?"

Justin's eyes snapped open. What a bizarre question. He had never known his mother to possess a metaphysical bent. Dog? God? He wasn't at all sure he *could* tell the difference.

He reached for his dog-god and stroked the long, curved back for reassurance.

"It's not bullying, is it?"

"*Not* bull-ee, burd-ee!" interrupted his brother, who had put down his toy monkey and begun flapping his arms like wings. "Fly!"

Justin turned to him, suspicious and discomfited by this suggestion (was it a suggestion?). He often had a feeling that Charlie knew more than he let on. The child smiled at him winningly.

Justin turned back to his mother. He assured her that bullying at school was not the problem. He was being bullied, all right, but not by some thicko schoolboy.

She was not reassured. "Stand still for a moment and let me look at you. I think you've developed a twitch."

Justin sighed, stood up, climbed the stairs, and locked himself in the bathroom.

He stayed there until the quiet click of toenails on wooden floor, a thump, and the reassuring sound of Boy snoring quietly in the hallway convinced him it was safe to come out.

I REALLY LIKE David.

No I don't. I don't give a damn about him.

I could run him down with a taxi. Give him a wasting disease.

Or worse, ignore him altogether. Let him live out his irrelevant little life in Luton with a dreary doting wife, two point four gormless children, and a ticking bomb for a heart.

But I do like a game now and again.

And he plays so nicely.

9

JUSTIN SURVIVED his first week at school.

With Boy at his side, he managed to act out his role as an average member of teenage society, albeit an increasingly isolated one. Friends gave up trying to engage him in conversation; his clothes were weird and he no longer answered to his name, a fact they found exceptionally irritating. A decreasing number of people bothered talking to him before school, sitting with him at the library, or asking when he was going to lunch. He hadn't realized his new identity would be so lonely.

Peter Prince, however, chose the shower next to his after PE. "Hey," he said cheerfully.

Justin looked up, grateful to be acknowledged. "Hey."

"Where's your dog?" Peter's voice came from within the gushing stream of water.

Justin thought he must have misheard. "Pardon?"

"Your dog."

"Yes?"

"Isn't he with you today?"

Justin looked at Peter. "Ha bloody ha."

Peter stuck his head out of the stream of water, features dripping. He smiled shyly. "I love greyhounds."

Justin stared. "My dog is imaginary."

"Oh." Peter looked interested. "That's unusual."

Justin put his head under the water. When he emerged, Peter was still looking at him.

"Less work," Peter offered, cheerily. "If the dog's imaginary, I mean. Not so much grooming, feeding, et cetera."

Justin continued to stare as Peter turned the massive old-fashioned tap to OFF, wrapped himself in a damp grayish towel the size of a dishrag, and dripped across the uneven tiled floor to his locker.

The following day, Peter fell into step with Justin as he walked home from school. Looking down to the approximate area of Justin's left heel, he smiled. "Hiya, boy."

Boy trotted over and leant against Peter briefly as Justin watched in wonder. The boundary between reality and fantasy wobbled dangerously.

Peter pulled a tennis ball out of his bag, threw it hard across the ground, and watched Boy chase after it. The dog sprang forward and shot off, moving so fast he blurred.

"Wow," Peter said happily, "what a beauty. Very ancient breed, you know. Kept by kings. Pharaohs used them to hunt lions."

Justin looked at him.

"Second only to cheetahs in speed. Huge hearts in relation to their weight; same size as ours."

Justin thought about this. Big hearts, long legs. All they needed was a slightly bigger brain and they'd rule the world. He kept walking, with his greyhound and Peter Prince lolloping at his side. "How do you know so much about greyhounds?"

Peter looked embarrassed. "I read a lot."

They walked in silence for a while, Peter contemplating greyhounds and Justin contemplating Peter. They didn't seem to have much in common. Did Peter imagine they might be friends? He'd had friends in the past, mainly based on mutual need—another person to kick a ball with, someone who had better toys at home. Peter appeared to be without motive in attaching himself to Justin and Boy. He seemed content just to keep them company.

At Justin's house, Peter waved and walked on. Justin stared after him but the other boy didn't look back.

Oh well, he thought. At least Boy likes him. The two might have been old friends, the way they fell in together.

But Boy's *my* dog!

Maybe it's a plot, he thought. Maybe they're working together. Maybe Peter is Boy's human spy contact, brought in as backup.

He looked at Boy. The dog had managed to wedge his narrow back under the kitchen radiator for warmth and was snoring contentedly.

Justin sighed. I can't even trust my own imaginary dog. How much lower can a person get?

10

SLOWLY, and in the absence of any competition, Justin began thinking of Peter as a friend. Peter wasn't exactly a social asset, but he was sympathetic and intelligent, and his dogged constancy appealed to Justin.

At school their friendship attracted attention, as pretty much everything did.

"Hey, look! It's Stephen Hawking and Head Case."

A pasty-faced group of younger boys sat on a wall outside the school gate at all hours of the day, stabbing limp, fatty chips with wooden forks and jeering at anything that moved.

Peter stopped and looked at them with clinical detachment.

"Sometimes I wonder how their brains work," he said, resuming his walk alongside Justin, "whether there's a mechanism by which serotonin is released in the process of attempting to demean others. It would explain a lot about the endemic nature of bullying."

"Maybe they're just cretins. Maybe they've been subjected to fetal dumb-ass syndrome in the womb."

Peter smiled. "Just as likely. Still, it makes you wonder."

"It makes *you* wonder."

As they passed another set of jeering boys, Peter stumbled, deftly knocking one of the ringleaders off the wall with his elbow. The boy fell backwards with a satisfying thump, unleashing a volley of abuse. Justin and Peter ran.

They slowed a few blocks later, laughing.

"Nice move," Justin said.

"Won't make him friendlier next time."

"You want to go back and rehabilitate him?"

Peter pulled the tennis ball out of his bag. As they stepped onto Luton common, he threw it along the ground for Boy. "I meant to ask you," he said, without turning to face Justin.

Boy brought the ball back and dropped it between the two boys. Peter threw it again, a long high arc. "What made you . . . I mean . . . why'd you change your name?"

Justin stopped. "It's a long story."

Boy caught the ball in midair halfway across the common, placed it carefully on the ground where he stood, and returned without it to the boys. Justin reached down to stroke his head. "Have you ever felt like fate has it in for you?"

"No," said Peter, frowning. "Have you?"

"Yes."

"That's strange." Peter thought for a moment, then looked

at Justin. "What does that have to do with changing your name?"

"It's part of my disguise."

"Your disguise?"

"My disguise from fate. I'm hiding."

"Hiding?"

"Yes."

"From fate?"

Justin nodded.

"Wow." Peter blinked at him. "You're serious?"

"Yes."

The silence lasted three-quarters of the way across the large expanse of withered grass.

"Interesting," Peter said slowly. "Of course I *have* thought rather a lot about predetermination, though perhaps not in exactly the way you mean. I sometimes get a feeling that something I remember hasn't actually happened yet, but I'm not sure whether it really *has* happened and I've just forgotten that it has."

He screwed up his face.

"I mean, if we accept that the universe is cylindrical and energy eventually joins up with itself, perhaps *thought* runs along the outside of the cylinder as well, repeating ad infinitum." He looked animated at the possibility. "That could mean that a thought actually *has* happened, in the sense of having taken place somewhere in the universe, along the outside of the cylinder, that is, but can't exactly be attributed to *me* as an individual. Or not yet, anyway."

Justin stared.

"Let's say, for instance, that you have the same dream over and over, only each time you're not sure whether you actually had the same dream before or just dreamt that you did." He looked at Justin expectantly. "It could relate to the thinning boundaries between *reality*, that is to say *active* expenditure of energy, and *thought*, or *passive* energy. Either way, the existence of the act, or in this case, the dream, is not in doubt. The question you have to ask is *how* does it exist, and how do we define the energy of thought versus the energy of action. You've posed a very interesting question here."

He paused.

"Take Boy here. I mean, does he exist or doesn't he? You see him, I see him. Is that enough to vouch for his existence? I would say it is. Surely there's a point at which an idea conjured by more than one brain has existence, not merely in the philosophical sense, but in the sense of being the *object* of expended energy. I'm quite interested in thought as energy, as valid an expression of energy as"—he paused, watching Boy race a squirrel to a tree—"as a running dog."

Boy granted the squirrel freedom and it spiraled, panicked, up to safety.

"It's not exactly what you'd call fate, perhaps. But possibly relevant in its way." Peter smiled apologetically.

Justin felt dazed by Peter's string of connections. His own brain soared and crashed, groped endlessly for elusive footholds in reality. There were dark corners he didn't dare enter, creaking catacombs lined with the corpses of doubt, incomprehension, and paranoia. His brain didn't grapple with theories, it grappled with *fear*.

They walked on in silence. A few hundred meters later where the road split, Justin stopped, wondering whether there was one last comment to be made. He couldn't think of one.

"Bye," he said.

Peter watched him go.

"Justin!"

Justin turned.

"I . . . I think you should meet my sister. She'd like you. I mean, you might like her, too." The embarrassed smile. "Anyway, you should meet."

Justin only nodded, but Peter looked pleased, as if something important had been settled.

Each boy headed home, deep in thought.

11

LIFE CONTINUED to pursue Justin. In his second week of school, as he made his way towards the changing rooms after PE, the athletics coach pulled him aside.

"Case!" Coach barked. "Ever thought about cross-country?"

Boy's ears flicked forward. He liked a good run.

Justin looked behind him.

"You, Case! Did you hear what I said?"

Justin nodded.

"Well? We need more runners this year."

"But I can't run."

"Bollocks," Coach spat. "Look at you. With a little training you could run all day."

Justin stared at Coach, amazed and suspicious. David Case

had never looked like a runner. It was one thing to change your shirts, quite another to assume an entirely different body type.

"Case!" Coach snapped impatiently. "You're not brain-dead, are you? That could disqualify you."

Justin shook his head: But I hate sport. And then: Perfect.

Coach rolled his eyes. "An answer, Case. Any answer will do."

"OK," said Justin. Boy wagged his tail.

Peter grinned when he heard. "You'll like it," he said. "Not at first, of course, it's horrible at first. But you get used to it eventually."

Justin didn't expect to like it, now or ever. Cross-country seemed a perverse sort of self-abuse consisting of endless grueling runs through the unattractive suburban landscape egged on by a wisecracking sadist whose life had repeatedly been blighted by mediocrity.

Coach's team had never captured a county championship. Coach himself had never discovered a future Olympic champion. No boy had ever returned to Luton Secondary years later to report that running had played a formative, nay, pivotal role in his life. The extra pay Coach received for three afternoons a week enduring the contempt and indifference of fifteen talentless teenage boys did not begin to compensate for the extent of his disenchantment.

Despite knowing all this, Justin was secretly pleased to have been plucked from athletic obscurity. No one had ever suggested he could run at all, much less all day. David Case was certainly no athlete, but Justin? Perhaps Justin was loaded with potential.

Without his noticing, he had already begun to change shape. Over the previous eighteen months he had grown six inches. His legs, always disproportionately long in relation to his torso, had lengthened further and his feet had grown two and a half sizes. But he was soft and slow, and it took a leap of faith to imagine he'd ever be anything different.

His first practice involved running at what felt like excessive speed along the school track, with Boy bounding easily around him in circles. After ten minutes he began to flag. Thirty minutes left him collapsed by the side of the track, gasping for air, legs shaking and contracted with cramp, lungs on fire, throat dry, stomach heaving. Boy licked his face once, then settled down next to him for a nap.

"Hey, you suck!" hissed one of his teammates.

One by one they passed, skimming around the gray outdoor track, each competing for the most hilariously entertaining insult.

"Hey, Granny."

"Puss puss pussy."

"Dickhead."

"Oi! Head Case!"

This last from Coach.

Justin barely noticed the insults. He was too busy trying to restore the flow of oxygen to his brain.

Peter said nothing as he flew past, but his silence exuded compassion.

Seven of the fifteen boys on Justin's team had been chosen for their ability to outrun the local constabulary; five others were blackmailed into participating, their academic potential so limited that alternative excuses had to be found to keep them in school. Most of this group whiled away unsupervised moments stopping for fags by the side of the track.

Justin didn't smoke, so he ran instead, discovering in the process that Coach had not been entirely wrong in his evaluation. Day by day he improved, modestly, steadily; soon he discovered a jawline and hard planes of muscle in his legs. He began to look different, rangy and fast, and best of all found he could run more or less indefinitely. His chest would eventually feel crushed under the strain of oxygen deprivation, at some point his muscles still pleaded with him to stop, but the pain took longer to set in, bothered him less, became familiar. He could keep up for longer periods and when he matched Peter stride for stride he felt triumphant.

His dog helped, loping gracefully by his side, lean and effortless. When Justin felt discouraged he concentrated on Boy's stylish gait, his noble spirit.

I am a greyhound, he thought as he ran, *I am king of dogs. I skim through time and space, travel at the speed of thought. The unknown is my prey, I bring it to earth in a single exquisite bound.*

He could feel the syncopation of his paws on the track, his narrow muzzle piercing the air, no sound except the pounding of his large, noble heart. He ran silently. He was an air hound, a sight hound, deadly in pursuit of a rabbit, a taut bow, a spinning arrow. For whole minutes at a time he was graceful, joyous.

The insults tailed off, at least from Coach.

"How'd I do?" Justin asked, panting, his legs shaking, body streaming with sweat.

"Jesus," Coach muttered, staring at his stopwatch. "Ten thousand meters in just under thirty-eight minutes."

Justin's chest swelled with pride. A few weeks ago he could barely stagger around the track.

It gave him hope. Perhaps whatever it was, he could outrun it.

12

JUSTIN WHISTLED.

Come on, Boy! Walkies!

Boy bounded over and jumped up on his master, nearly knocking him over. He was a big dog, nearly a meter at the shoulder. Justin rubbed behind his ears. Nice Boy.

Out of the corner of his eye, he saw his mother watching him out of the corner of her eye.

What's the matter, he thought peevishly. Hadn't she ever seen an imaginary dog?

She appeared anxious, perhaps about the safety of his little brother in the presence of such a large animal, though Charlie showed no sign of fear. Anyway, surely he, Justin, was entitled to a pet of his own choosing. Come to think of it, why hadn't she and his father provided one? Maybe if he'd had a real dog, he wouldn't feel so threatened.

Then again, maybe not.

Justin wanted to see Agnes again, but his desire was tempered with uncertainty. He was young, not suave or knowing. Not brilliant or sexually irresistible. He had quite a handsome dog, but it didn't exist. In short, he didn't add up to much.

Which made it all the more surprising when, a little more than a month after they first met, Agnes phoned him.

"Justin Case, at last. There are twelve Cases in the phone book; your number happens to be the eleventh."

Justin was struck dumb.

"Hello? Are you there?"

"I just . . . it's just . . ." Perfect, he thought, I've developed a speech impediment.

"Never mind, I need to see you. I'll meet you in ten minutes at the café on West Street."

Agnes hung up.

Justin stared at the receiver. Why had she phoned? Perhaps he had amnesia. Perhaps he and Agnes often met at the café to chat about . . . about international economic destabilization.

His life seemed to be getting away from him.

He entered the café.

"Table for one?" asked the waitress with an air of resentment.

"Two." His voice warbled slightly.

She pointed at a table wedged between the toilet and the kitchen. He ignored it, choosing a booth in the corner with a view of the street, sat down, and ordered a cup of tea. By sipping in infinitesimal increments, he made it last nearly the entire half hour during which Agnes did not show. Doubt and self-loathing took root in his brain. He was about to pay his meager bill and crawl into the street howling with psychic pain when he saw her pink bob, bob-bobbing along outside the window. Today she was disguised as a geisha in a brightly colored kimono, short green felt culottes, white foundation, huge dark glasses, and six-inch platform clogs. Over one shoulder hung a striped plastic portfolio.

She threw him a kiss through the window and entered the café. Justin slumped in his seat, embarrassed to have been kept waiting.

Agnes arrived at the table, amused. "Hello, Justin Case. I'm terribly sorry I'm late."

"Hello." He looked at the floor.

She stood very still until he looked up again, then slipped the glasses down her nose and stared straight into his eyes, smiling the smallest, most seductive of smiles. "I am *extremely* pleased to see you."

"I . . . ," he began, but found he couldn't go on. He reached for Boy, and gathered the warm elastic skin of his dog's neck in one hand.

I wonder if I'm in love, he thought. Or if she is?

At his feet, Boy raised one eyebrow and gazed up at his master.

Justin waited as Agnes settled herself daintily into the seat opposite, waved a tiny handkerchief patterned with cherry blossoms, and ordered chamomile tea with the demure, murmuring voice of a geisha. When she finally turned to him, she reminded him of some blank-faced exotic bug. It made him nervous not to see her eyes.

She picked the portfolio off the floor, laid it flat on the table between them, and leant in close. "I'm sorry it's taken me so long to print these up. But"—here she paused for dramatic effect and lowered her voice to a whisper—"it was *worth the wait*."

Beneath the table, Boy rolled over onto one side, stretched ostentatiously, closed both eyes, and began to snore. Agnes opened the portfolio, slid out four large proof sheets, placed them in front of Justin, and sat back in her chair.

He picked up the first.

The boy in the pictures was slim, almost scraggy. His hair was longish, his skin very pale. In a frame marked with an "x," he had his hands crammed into the front pockets of his jeans. His body was in profile and he appeared to have turned to look at the camera only an instant before. His expression was suspicious, anxious, slightly blurred.

It was a long moment before Justin realized he was looking at himself.

"Well?" said Agnes.

"Well, what?"

"Well, what do you *think*? Isn't it amazing?"

Amazing wasn't the word he would have chosen. He looked like someone else entirely. Someone pale, anxious, and well dressed. Considering his mission, it was thrilling. Considering everything else it was deeply disturbing.

"That's not what I look like."

She beamed at him, triumphant. "It *wasn't*. Until I saw you."

He thought about this. "So what will you do with them?" he asked finally, riffling through the sheaf of proofs.

"They're not important. You are. I can't believe I found you in deepest Luton."

Justin winced.

"Don't look so frightened. You don't actually have to *do* anything. You're perfect the way you are."

What way am I?

"But before I take more pictures, there's somewhere we need to go. When are you available?"

He was always available. He looked at Agnes. Did she want to have sex with him? Did he want to have sex with her?

"Where are we going?"

"London."

London? You could hardly get more dangerous than that. Kigali, maybe. Or Baghdad. He glanced up at Agnes, who was calmly flipping through her diary as if entering the heart of urban darkness were the sort of thing she did casually, without considering the consequences—the international terrorists, homicidal taxi drivers, care-in-the-community cases let loose to push unsuspecting out-of-towners under trains.

He shuddered.

"How about nine a.m. Saturday week at the station?"

Having no diary and no previous engagements, Justin said yes.

13

LONG BEFORE EINSTEIN thought up his theory of relativity, any child could explain that some days passed more slowly than others and some weeks dragged pretty much into eternity.

The ten days between Justin's two meetings with Agnes moved with as much directional momentum as a satellite tumbling in deep space. There were times when he sat in class staring at the huge black and white institutional clock, drifted off into a long reverie about his tragic demise in the concrete jungle or his future sexual prospects, and awoke hours later to find the hands in exactly the same position as before. It defied the laws of something or other, something he might have known more about had he paid attention during physics. Instead, he settled into a stalled world devoid of linear motion and gave up all hope that the day he longed for and feared in equal measure would ever arrive.

A quarter of a second later it did.

Justin awoke the morning of their meeting, pulled an ancient green anorak over his new clothes, inserted himself back into the swiftly moving stream of ordinary time, and set off to meet Agnes.

Luton was not a big town, and it took less than fifteen minutes to walk to the station. As he walked, he fantasized about their day, rehearsed once again in his head for what had become, in the intervening period, a series of profoundly erotic possibilities. This line of thought forestalled more familiar and disturbing ones, the ones that involved being kidnapped by Estonian mafiosi, blown up by animal rights activists, repeatedly stabbed by a bus driver with a grudge. Each of the last ten nights he had floated off into a semi-dreamworld in which Agnes couldn't keep her hands off him; each night their interaction became more elaborate, more erotically complex. At some point reality and fantasy switched places so that his dream life became more vivid than his real one.

But now, in the harsh light of day, doubts crept in. Could the lure of sex overcome his fear of danger? And what exactly *were* his prospects in that quarter? Agnes seemed to like him well enough, but how much was that? A little? A lot? Enough to have sex with him on a train?

He imagined meeting her, imagined her red-eyed and flustered on the platform; imagined her face brightening at his arrival. He imagined them alone in the small, old-fashioned compartment, the train half empty. She would confess her unhappiness. In his mind, casual affection became suppressed passion; she would admit lying awake all night, unable to sleep, burning with desire for . . . for . . .

He stopped at a corner, waited for the traffic to notice him, and crossed.

She'd be suddenly shy.

A bomb would . . . no!

He imagined himself masterful, seductive.

Then she would look at him in a certain pleading way and at that moment, no words would be necessary. Her mouth would soften and her eyes widen, and she would lift her hand to his cheek, and then he would kiss her, softly at first and then passionately, harder than she might have expected from someone young and inexperienced like him, kiss her until she pulled away and begged him, *Justin, don't.* But he wouldn't listen, and she wouldn't really want him to, and one thing would lead to another and then he would be pulling open the buttons of her shirt, pushing up her skirt, sliding his hand up between her thighs to feel the soft warm curve of her, her, you know.

He jostled a young woman, sending her mobile phone crashing to the pavement. "Excuse me," he muttered as she glared at him. He hurried on, head down.

Agnes would look at him hungrily, moan in his arms, *Oh god, Justin, stop, we can't, you're too young!* but they would not stop. He could feel her lips on his ear, whispering in a voice strangely coarse:

Oooh, Justin, ram it to me hard—

WHACK.

And then he was on the ground, disorientated and half-conscious. For a moment he felt no pain at all, but a few seconds later it made its appearance, radiating outwards from his forehead, now so intense it made his stomach heave. He had to lie down to stop himself pitching headlong on the wildly spinning ground.

Oh god, he thought feebly, *that voice!*

A crowd began to gather. Boy whimpered and rested his muzzle in the crook of Justin's neck.

Justin thought: A sniper. I've been shot.

He struggled to a sitting position, feeling for the sticky wetness oozing from a bullet hole in his forehead. Someone's hands were behind him, on his shoulders, supporting him gently. He forced his eyes to focus, desperately sweeping the crowd for the hit man, the smoking gun tossed away in the gutter.

There was nothing. No blood. No bullet hole. No murder weapon. Nothing, except . . .

A lamppost.

He had walked into an iron lamppost. The impact had nearly knocked his face through the back of his head.

An old lady prodded him with her walking stick. "What's the matter, moron, you blind?"

Behind Justin a younger girl, soft-featured and sturdy with thick brown hair and the same eyes as Peter, supported him until he could sit up on his own. She stood for a moment, head slightly cocked, listening to the silent whir of confusion that emanated from his brain like a badly played song.

No wonder he walks into things, she thought.

Then she leaned down, gave Boy a pat, smoothed her skirt over grazed, chubby knees, and slipped into a pocket of the crowd. She wondered when their paths would cross again.

Back on the pavement, time slowed to a wow-wowing 15 rpm as Justin accepted the arm of a stocky middle-aged woman with a stroller, stood up shakily and, with his dog at his side, resumed his journey.

14

AT THE STATION he described the incident to Agnes. She examined the lump on his head.

"You didn't just accidentally walk into a lamppost?"

"Yes, of course." Justin was impatient. "But it wasn't just me, I felt *him*, he was *directing me*. I heard his voice."

"What did he say?"

Justin avoided her eyes. "I don't remember. But it was horrible. Like he was jeering at me."

"You sure it wasn't just some kid walking nearby?"

"You think I'm suffering from aural hallucinations?" His throbbing head made him cross.

"Don't put words in my mouth."

The train pulled onto the track with a screech.

"Come on," she said. "This is us."

The car was too crowded for them to sit together. Justin felt relieved. It wasn't the moment for a seduction. Not with a purple lump the size of a baby's fist growing out of his forehead.

He gazed through the window at the desultory stretch of countryside that lay between Luton and London. From across the carriage he could hear the click click click of Agnes's camera.

I spy a condominium. I spy a mad cow. I spy a field full of pesticides. I spy a bird with a broken wing. I spy . . .

He spied a bedraggled old donkey standing motionless in a chewed-over field, its back swayed, its head drooping. To his horror, he felt his eyes fill with tears.

In the reflection of the window he could see a girl staring at him.

He turned to the seat diagonally across and glanced nervously at its occupant. She had short thick legs, a short thick torso, pale blond hair, and large pixie ears. She had unfolded a map of London and stretched it out on the huge rucksack that leaned on her knee. She smiled at him.

"Excuse me," she said in heavily accented English. "Do you know how I will be finding Victoria Station?"

Justin took the map she offered and studied it carefully. He had no better idea how to get around London than she had, but felt a host's obligation to offer assistance.

"I'm afraid I don't know," he said at last, handing it back.

"Maybe together we can be finding it, yes?" She looked up at him through pale thin lashes.

"I'm with my friend," Justin explained weakly, pointing at Agnes.

The girl craned her neck to get a look at the competition. Agnes smiled encouragingly and photographed them both. The girl turned back to Justin, disappointed.

"Oh well. Next time maybe?"

Justin nodded as they pulled into the station. He jumped up and squeezed past the transfer passengers with their huge suitcases, catching up with Agnes on the platform.

"So," she said. "Who's your girlfriend?"

"You mean Frodo?"

"Don't be cruel. She fancied you. It's working."

"What's working?"

"Your transformation. Soon they'll be flocking to you like—"

"Like what? Vultures? Vampires? Penguins?"

She headed for the station exit. "This way. We can walk from here."

"Where are we going?"

In answer, she took his hand and quickened her pace.

Agnes led Justin through the maze of grim dingy streets around the station, until they came to a narrow opening between two houses. A sign on the crumbling brick wall read STABLE LANE. It was the perfect setting for a toothless muscle-bound villain with piano wire to garrote them both and eviscerate the bodies, leaving a mass of tangled guts spilling out onto the cold ground.

"This is it," Agnes said, stopping at the door of a gloomy building, unmarked except for a flickering orange neon OO in the first-floor window, the remnants of a sign originally advertising ROOMS. Agnes rang the bell, waited for the soft buzz, and entered, followed by Justin.

Inside was a narrow staircase. They climbed to a landing and pushed through a heavy iron door which opened into a large, low-ceilinged room wallpapered in dark silk. The room was dense with color and pattern and hung with such massive gilded French Baroque mirrors that the eye was fooled into thinking it extended infinitely in every direction. On the wide, oak floors lay oriental carpets; on the carpets stood racks of clothing. Light from hundreds of little halogen bulbs twinkled in the ceiling like stars.

Justin felt as if he'd stepped into an old-fashioned Easter egg. The place smelled of something exotic and expensive, like the hold of a ship en route from the West Indies. Clove, he thought. Frankincense. Cinnamon.

It took a moment for his eyes to adjust to the tiny lights reflected and multiplied in the mirrors. Now he could see members of a strange species of female creature swiveling around the room, some in jeans and platform heels, some in brightly colored suits or dresses, but all oddly tall and oddly self-possessed, their hair exaggerated and their legs unnaturally long. They had staring eyes and fat engorged lips. They giggled and gossiped, but their expressions froze into masks of disdain when they noticed Justin.

"Models," whispered Agnes. "They appeared the day this place opened. Like ants at a picnic. No one knows how they do it."

Oh god, Justin thought, fashion again. Why not something simple, like Sanskrit or statistics?

Agnes took his arm and led him across the room. Standing at a long wooden worktable, face averted, was a tall endomorph with a perfect oblong head and the meditative air of a Tibetan monk. He wore softly tailored black trousers and a thick charcoal cardigan unraveled at all its edges so that individual strands of wool reached nearly to the floor. Guessing at his country of origin, Justin chose a handful: Japan, France, India. When the man turned towards them, Justin saw that his eyes were hard and sharp as broken glass.

"Hello, Ivan," Agnes said.

The man kissed her on both cheeks. "Welcome, as always, dear girl." Dipping his head, he indicated the customers with a narrowing of his eyes. "Please excuse the mess."

Agnes suppressed a smile. "Yes, of course. You appear to be thriving."

"I make a living." Ivan shrugged. Despite the exotic appearance, his English was without accent.

Agnes stepped closer, lowered her voice, and inclined her head in Justin's direction. "Ivan, look at this boy I found."

Justin winced. *This boy I found.* Like an old glove on the pavement.

"Well?" Her voice was soft. "What do you think?"

Ivan looked, examining Justin with the clinical detachment of someone who has seen far too many exceptional faces. He raised an elegant tapered finger to his own forehead and looked questioningly at Agnes.

"The bump is temporary," she said.

Ivan turned back to Justin. "Yes," he said finally. And then again, "Yes."

Justin huddled into his anorak and began to back away.

Placing a firm hand on his shoulder, Agnes stopped him. "Ivan, this is my friend, Justin Case."

"Welcome." With grim formality, Ivan bowed slightly to Justin. "To what do I owe the honor?"

"He needs . . . finishing."

Ivan nodded. "Yes, of course." He stifled a yawn.

"Ivan's got a wonderful eye," Agnes whispered.

Justin imagined an all-seeing eyeball shoved deep in the man's trouser pocket, damp and slimy like a squid.

Across the room, a girl appeared from a dressing room in a layered owl-shaped dress that failed completely to enhance her emaciated beauty. Her friend beamed approval.

Justin stared.

"So," Ivan said to Agnes, studying Justin and rolling a black button between his fingers. "Not a suit. A coat, perhaps?"

"Whatever you think. Something impressive. I'm photographing him."

Ivan frowned. "I might have something."

He disappeared, returning a few minutes later carrying a long ice gray shearling coat with black buttons. He held it carelessly draped over one arm and smacked it a few times. Justin watched small clouds of dust rise from it; Ivan's hand left a slightly paler mark on the surface of the suede.

"The cut is too narrow to suit anyone who might afford it. Men with money are rarely slim."

Justin stared at the coat. It looked like the illegitimate issue of a yak and a football.

Ivan caught his expression and shrugged. "Take it or not."

"It'll be completely different on," said Agnes, taking the coat from Ivan and holding it out for Justin.

Wondering exactly how different it would have to be, Justin turned, held out his arms, and allowed Agnes to slip it on.

He blushed. He suspected he looked like a lunatic, but the truth was that the coat fit; it was much lighter and softer than it looked and he felt wonderfully cosseted in its shaggy warmth. Justin turned to face Agnes, who pushed him in the direction of a huge gold mirror. One of the models swiveled past, plucked at his sleeve, and made an appreciative noise.

Justin looked at himself. Then at Agnes, on whose face a tiny smile had appeared.

"It's good."

And God pronounced that it was good, thought Justin.

"Ivan," Agnes called, "it's perfect."

Justin felt his face burn. There was no way he could afford a coat like this, even if he'd wanted it. He turned away, furious, but Agnes grabbed his arm, speaking softly into his ear. "Forget it, Justin. You don't have to pay. It's the new barter economy. Plus," she said, "the pictures I take of you are worth far more than any coat. Go on, take it."

"I don't want it." Justin tore the coat off and thrust it at her. "Take it back."

She looked at him mildly. "You heard Ivan, it will never fit anyone rich enough to buy it. You may as well have it."

She carried the coat across the room to Ivan, who wrapped it carefully in black tissue paper, placed it in a shopping bag the color of heavy cream, and held it out to Justin with a neutral expression. He even bowed slightly, and Justin felt certain he was being mocked.

Agnes took the bag. "Thank you, Ivan."

Ivan's face was composed, expressionless. "He'll pay me back someday."

She looked at him. "What do you mean?"

"What I said." Ivan shrugged. The soft oval of his face reorientated itself away from them and then back, like a periscope.

Justin retreated, arms crossed protectively across his chest, humming to tune out their conversation.

After a minute or two, he noticed that the room had gone silent. He looked over to find Ivan and Agnes staring at him. Agnes's expression was solemn.

"I hope you don't mind, Justin. I've been telling Ivan about the fate thing."

Ivan looked more interested than before. The longer he stared, the more uneasy Justin felt. His eye twitched.

Finally Ivan spoke, so softly that Justin had to move closer to make out the words.

"I have observed fate," he said.

Justin's heart began to pound with alarm. They were less than an arm's length apart now, so close that Justin could smell the other man's skin. A hint of something expensive rose from it.

"And I can tell you for certain," Ivan crooned as Agnes watched, rapt, "you *are* doomed."

Justin couldn't breathe.

"In your life," Ivan said softly, "you will suffer *inestimable* losses. And then you, too, will die, causing inestimable pain to others. And all this will happen to you, *not if, but when.*"

Justin swayed slightly.

"*That* is the only truth you need to know about fate."

Justin struggled away from the seductive voice. "Let's *go,*" he said to Agnes.

"But—"

"*NOW.*"

He grabbed her arm but she pulled free, so he went alone, slamming the iron door behind him with a crash.

"Goodbye, Justin Case," Ivan called, his face lit by an unpleasant smile. "And *good luck.*"

At the bottom of the stairs, Justin fumbled with the catch on the outside door and stumbled out into the narrow lane, heart pounding as if he'd run for miles. Agnes caught him up, and he spun around like a cornered animal, grabbing her shoulders.

"He's *horrible.*"

"Yes, I know. But his clothes are fantastic. And he can be very generous when he feels like it." She pulled free and dug through the layers of tissue paper. "Here, put the coat on and tell me how you feel."

She held it out to him, her expression soft. "Please, Justin. Please?"

It was a standoff and he didn't particularly want to win, so he took the coat and slipped it on. Boy sniffed it and growled, smelling goat, as Agnes clicked off a series of shots: Justin Embarrassed. Justin Startled. Justin Angry.

Justin turned away from the flash.

"Excellent," Agnes murmured, taking his arm and steering him back out to the main road towards a tiny run-down Indian restaurant with flashing fairy lights in the window. "Now let's celebrate."

Through the supple skin of the sleeve, the pressure of her fingers caused him to shiver.

15

JUSTIN WORE HIS NEW COAT like a second skin. It protected him, kept him warm, yet was eccentric enough to satisfy his new identity. Inside it he felt safe, and he took it off only to sleep or run, activities that increasingly consumed his life.

Peter had been right about running. It wasn't long before pleasure began to dominate pain. Justin had never considered himself athletic, but now, as he offered encouragement to his lungs and limbs, they rose like Titans on the field of battle.

My body! He thought gratefully. It works!

Often when he ran he lost touch with his physical limitations and began to cruise, aligning his heartbeat to the beat of his feet on the tarmac.

How could he not have known this was possible?

He wasn't particularly competitive. What he liked was the steady, reassuring tempo that regulated the surges of anxiety in his brain. Tick tock tick tock. His body fell into the mechanical rhythm of an old-fashioned alarm clock.

The more he ran, the less like David Justin felt.

These aspects of running were lost on his coach, who merely shouted at his team with increased resignation as competition loomed.

On a grim Tuesday afternoon in late October, six schools' worth of shivering boys huddled in a drizzle, awaiting the starter's signal. Justin had invited Agnes to attend, in a way that made clear how little he cared whether she did or didn't, and how little he expected her to.

As he approached the start, something caused him to look up. Following the direction of a hundred other pairs of eyes, he turned to see Agnes walking towards them under a huge lilac umbrella covered in bright polka dots, her feet steady on the soggy turf in a pair of green rubber knee-high wellies, her camera bag swinging from one shoulder. The rest of her was shrink-wrapped in what looked like cellophane. She looked preposterous. Sublime.

The entire event paused, stunned, as Agnes made her way across the field to the makeshift wooden observers' stand. On arrival, she furled her umbrella and sat, to a ripple of spontaneous applause. She smiled at Justin and pulled her Nikon from the camera bag, followed by a single white glove. She waved the glove in the direction of the team.

Peter waved back happily. Justin turned away to hide the expression on his face.

Collecting its scattered wits, the meet continued.

Justin had no recollection of the starting gun. When next he noticed the outside world, he was running, or at least his body was. He was intrigued to discover that his feet came with cruise control. He didn't have to think about what he was doing, just set them on "fast" and they ran.

Boy bounded ahead in a playful mood. Occasionally he would stop to look back at the seething, panting mass of boys with something like pity.

Perhaps you people should stick to something at which you excel, said the look.

Then he would fly off again, his body airborne for most of the length of his stride. He ran joyful circles around the leaders, accelerated to a mile a minute for the pure fun of it, crossed the finish line to the sound of his own ovation, spun around, and returned to Justin's side where he slowed to an encouraging canter. Beneath the aristocratic condescension of his breed he was kind.

Directly to Justin's left and a few meters ahead ran Peter Prince. He turned back and glanced at Justin, falling off the pace slightly as he did. Justin barely noticed. At the halfway mark, his mind was on Agnes. She had swept his protests away as if it were nothing to give some boy you barely knew a fantastically expensive coat as a gift. The next time she'd phoned, his determination to remain distant had been crushed by the purring intimacy of her voice.

Surely it all meant something. Something more than just "you're not bad, as kids go." He recognized the existence of a code, a secret language of the initiated that allowed them to translate the nuances of sexual intent. Her continued presence in his life must say something about her intentions. But what?

A voice very close to his ear whispered words he couldn't quite hear and with a jolt he was reunited with his body. Running so fast hurt. He turned to see who had whispered. He could feel the horrible soft impression of breath on his ear like a dusty flapping moth. He brushed it away with his hand, panicky, but there was nothing there.

Then the voice came again, whispery, urgent.

Run!

Justin bolted. Panting, he pulled ahead of Peter, who looked puzzled at the expression on his friend's face.

Run, run, as fast as you can!

Boy had moved in and now ran as close to Justin as possible. Justin ignored him, hurtling forwards, blind with terror.

One hundred meters from the finish line. The rest of the contenders made whatever moves they had left.

Justin couldn't see or hear them, didn't realize they were there. He heard only the voice in his ear and ran as fast as he could.

RUN!

He crossed the line first and kept running. Boy gently guided him into a curve, leaning his full weight against Justin's hip as a brake.

Coach looked pleased.

It was a genuine moment of glory. His first. But he felt queasy, violated. Adrenaline continued to pump to his brain, his stomach heaved with fear, his pulse failed to drop below racing peak.

Run, run, as fast as you can.

Peter caught up and thumped him on the back happily. With him was a girl of about eleven, with thick brown hair and her brother's clear, fearless eyes.

"This is my sister, Dorothea," Peter said.

The girl stared at Justin, recognizing the look on his face from an earlier encounter. There was no lamppost this time, but it didn't seem to matter.

Justin looked straight through her.

That voice.

He remembered the end of the nursery rhyme now.

You can't catch me, I'm the gingerbread man.

16

BY THE TIME JUSTIN WALKED through the front door, the phone was ringing.

"Justin!" Agnes trilled. "You were brilliant today. I was madly impressed."

He was silent.

"Justin? What's the matter?"

"I need to see you."

"Now?"

"Now."

He put down the phone. Charlie had appeared at his feet and he pulled the child up onto his lap. The little boy wrapped his arms around Justin's neck.

"I won a race today," Justin told him softly. "It was horrible."

Charlie tightened his grip and murmured urgently into his brother's ear. Justin couldn't make out the words, but the little boy's tone was soothing and full of love. They sat that way for a minute, and then Justin stood up to leave, carefully disengaging the child's arms. Charlie toddled over to the window and pressed his face against it, gazing after the figure of the older boy as he closed the front door and disappeared down the road.

This time it was Justin who arrived second at the café. As he crossed the room towards Agnes, she couldn't help experiencing a small surge of pride at her creation. Justin looked taller, fitter, more graceful. The soft gray coat hung lightly from his shoulders. Even his anxiety seemed more compelling than before: darker, less twitchy. In different circumstances she might even have fancied him herself.

Justin caught her glint of triumph and for an instant saw himself through her eyes. Pygmalion's Galatea. Dr. Frankenstein's monster.

Justin sat and Agnes peered at him closely. "So what's this about?"

"I heard something."

"What sort of thing?"

"The voice."

"Ah. What did it say this time?"

"It told me to run."

She was silent for a moment. "You're sure it was Fate, or Doom or whatever?"

"Run, run, as fast as you can, you can't catch me, I'm the gingerbread man."

"Ooh, creepy." Agnes looked impressed. "Did it mean run away?"

"I don't know what it means." He shivered, and she put a hand on his arm.

"I don't believe in stuff like this as a rule. But it does sound weird."

Justin sat wreathed in gloom, as Agnes waved to the waitress and ordered tea. Then she looked at him carefully. "Aside from the voices, how are you?"

"OK, I guess. I get a lot of strange looks at school."

"Good strange or bad strange?"

"Both." He sighed.

"Are you complaining?"

Justin looked glum. "Not exactly. Only, I guess I was hoping . . ."

She waited.

"I was hoping to feel better. Safer."

"And you don't?"

"Even when I'm not hearing voices, or imagining being murdered by snipers, I feel like a blinking neon sign. When girls look at me I feel like the cheese in a mousetrap."

"There's a word for that, Justin. Lust. It means they fancy you. It's because you look good."

She met his eyes and for a fleeting instant experienced a whirring sensation in her blood. Then she raised her camera and clicked off a shot. Portrait.

"It's supposed to feel good," she said gently. "It's supposed to make you feel desirable."

Justin looked at her. "It's not *me* they want. It's some strange hybrid-me made up of new clothes and insomnia."

"Look, Justin, you're fifteen for Christ's sake. What do you want? Everyone changes. I wore Moroccan gowns with African combs in my hair when I was fifteen."

"It's not all about style."

She groaned. "Don't tell *me* what it's all about, Mr. Wisdom of the Ages. *I* know it's not all about style. You're the one who wanted a new identity. *I'm* the one who every once in a blue moon suggests that Fate isn't some middle-aged man with a squint who won't recognize you if you change your clothes."

She glared at him.

"Jesus, Justin. I don't believe in any of this stuff anyway. But you're not an idiot or schizophrenic as far as I can tell, so I listen. Do I believe there's some supernatural force out to get you? Look at it from my point of view. I never believed in the tooth fairy. This doesn't seem a good place to start."

He managed a rather formal smile and stood up to leave. "Thank you for listening to me, Agnes. I know I'm a pain."

"Sit down, for god's sake, don't run away." But she felt the flaw between them, the imperfect connection.

Agnes opened her bag and handed him an oversized magazine printed on heavy matte paper. "Take this, anyway," she said. "It's just out today."

He rolled the magazine up like a weapon and left the café. Halfway home, he dropped it in a bin.

Agnes watched him go and sighed. Such an exasperating boy. Exasperating, too, that it was beyond her powers to put him right.

17

AT SCHOOL THE NEXT DAY, a girl approached Justin. She was dark-haired and beautiful, with a scornful pout and perfect almond eyes. His peripheral vision automatically searched for her sniggering cronies lurking in a corner.

She carried an oversized magazine pressed flat against her chest like a shield.

"You're Justin, aren't you." She spoke without inflection, looking everywhere in the room but at him.

"Yes."

"Great pictures, Justin."

What pictures?

She spoke to the opposite wall this time. "So. You going to Angel's party?"

Justin blinked.

"Well," she repeated, slightly annoyed, "you *going*?"

He stared at the girl. She had the most agonizingly seductive, contemptuous eyes.

"I don't even know your name."

"Shireen." She sighed impatiently.

How perfectly the name suited her: shimmery and sheer, sensuous, serene.

"So?" She gazed at the ceiling with irritation, flicking her nails.

He was desperate to say yes, go to the party, bring her alcoholic punch in a plastic cup, walk home with her afterwards in the cold night air, offering his coat and putting his arm around her shoulders for warmth. He was desperate to dance with her, kiss her goodnight when they reached her door, press his virgin lips to her silky pink mouth; he was desperate to see her again, make a date for coffee, the cinema. He wanted to sit close to her in the dark, breathe the flowery female scent of her, feel the brush of her glossy hair against his face; he wanted to nuzzle her neck, tell her he loved her and then slip his hand inside her padded push-up bra, stroke the delicate skin of her breast, feel the crinkly nipple between his fingers. He gasped, and shoved a hand in his pocket, pressing his quivering erection flat against his groin.

Boy growled.

"*No.*"

The word erupted from somewhere near his solar plexus: half suspicion, half alarm. He didn't trust her. She was booby-trapped. Wired to explode in his face. A Venus land mine.

"Thanks anyway," he added, eyes glued to a poster just behind her describing the Heimlich maneuver.

Shireen stalked off, shoulders hunched in furious humiliation.

Justin went home and changed into sweats. It was drizzling; the pavements shone with oily water, reflecting images of the miserable suburban street. He called Boy, who lifted his head far enough to see the thin curtain of gray rain, then put it down again.

"Sill-ee-Boy!" chortled his brother.

Justin looked at Charlie impatiently. "Oh yeah? Well, what would you have done?"

The startled child gathered his thoughts.

I'm not entirely sure what the circumstances are, he said, but as a general rule I try to keep things simple. If I'm clear about what I want, other people have an easier time making me happy. It sounds basic, but most of the time it works.

"Duck." He spoke clearly, pointing to a wooden duck.

Automatically, Justin got up and fetched the duck.

"See?" said Charlie with a satisfied smile.

As if a one-year-old could sort out his problems, Justin thought. He patted his brother's head and left the room, trailing self-pity like a snail.

Charlie looked at the duck and sighed.

Justin closed the front door behind him and set off, making a point to stamp in every puddle as he ran along. He needed the sensation of shattering house after house until the only structures left in his neighborhood were abstract shiny fragments of brick and pebbledash.

The filthy rainwater soaked into his sneakers and socks but he didn't notice. You run today, he said to his legs, to his thighs, his buttocks his ankles his elbows his torso, his shoulders and knees. You get on with the mechanics, I've got things to think about.

His body, eager to be of service, obeyed.

Somewhere quietly in the background, he heard the steady beat beat beat of his feet on the pavement, reliable and automatic.

In the foreground his thoughts floated free, riding his body's wake as it flew through the outskirts of Luton.

For a while he let his eyes half close and felt the damp breeze cooling his feverish brain. He tried to empty it, pull the plug on the humiliations of the day and let them flood out behind him onto the street like bathwater. And then slowly, gradually, he began to inhale thoughts to fill it again. He breathed in deeply through his nose, and into the empty cave of his skull flowed the swirling vapors of people, ideas, desires.

He inhaled Agnes, fluorescent lime and sparkly. He was her TV makeover project, the one where a SWAT team revamps your kitchen, bathroom, garden, wardrobe, sex life. In hope and desperation, he had given her his brief for a new body and soul, and she was doing her best to comply. It wasn't her fault the experiment was a failure.

Agnes wasn't disdainful; he was convinced her affection for him was at least partially genuine. It was the *why* that puzzled him. Perhaps to her, he was the ultimate charity case, malleable, desperate, and faintly entertaining. She obviously wasn't interested in him, interested in *that way*. Was she? Could sexual feeling be totally one-sided? While he ached with lust, was she thinking about shoelaces?

There was so much he didn't know.

He thought about Peter, cheerful as chocolate, forever coasting on some gentle equatorial current. What *was* it about Peter? What clause of exemption allowed him to be gawky, uncool, *and* invulnerable?

Then there was fate, that soft presence, the seducer at the edge of the abyss, lulling him into a comfortable sense of security, luring him into the path of danger, then snatching him out, enticing him into a shell game he was guaranteed to lose. He felt worn out from turning left when he meant to go right, saying no instead of yes.

And yet. If he stepped on a crack . . .

His life stretched before him like some diabolical obstacle course. The mines had been hidden, dug deep into the ground. He merely had to predict their positions and avoid blowing himself to kingdom come.

He left the pavement and began to run along the verge. The uneven surface caused him to stumble.

Think about something else. Something pleasant.

He thought about Shireen's peculiar come-on. He inhaled the thought of his encounter with her, gold, fragrant, and heavy with the incense of ambiguity. He concentrated hard, letting her fill him, pushing fate out of his brain, replacing its gloomy miasma with her imperious sexual buzz. In his head he explored her body, ran his hand down the sensuous curve of her contempt, closed his eyes and buried his face in the sullen, silky weight of her indifference. He let his heart pump her bright aura through his veins like morphine, like adrenaline, warming and energizing the machine, causing it to glide, accelerate.

There was no affection in his recollection of their encounter, no fantasy that they would walk hand in hand sharing little jokes and pet names. Instead, he fast-forwarded to the party where they might have danced sweatily to some trendy DJ. He'd have taken her hand and led her through the teeming crowd to a quieter place, a bedroom where they would fumble for each other, igniting something panting and desperate and then follow it through, not to the point of humiliation and terror, but far enough to make him feel less like a huge pulsing pink neon sign reading VIRGIN.

Sprinting, panting, exhausted, he felt the final shreds of gilded cloud dissipate, leaving him alone, a lost boy in a bleak landscape, his brain weighed down with the grim reality of his life. It wasn't Shireen he was interested in anyway. Almost any girl, it seemed, could cause his body to respond, inspire a spasm of grateful sexual desire. He was at the mercy of the entire female sex. His weakness made him vulnerable to the worst sort of danger. He would enter the swamp like a blind man, slip slowly down into the sucking whirlpool of the unknown, waving. Drowning.

He stopped running, finally, hands on knees, breathing hard, checked his watch, and waited while his brain drifted back into his body. He felt the pain dripping down his left hamstring, chest heaving, face hot, feet sodden and blistering.

He had left Luton behind, reached the outskirts of Toddington. Twelve miles. It was pouring now. All around him the world was slowly turning to mud. Tired and soaked, he began limping back home.

18

SHIREEN WENT TO ANGEL'S PARTY with Alex. Alex had a car, plenty of confidence, and no brain to speak of. He was definitely not gay.

Alex and Shireen could have been matched by class vote, so compatible were their vital statistics: identical good looks, identical social status, identical attitudes of genetic superiority in the face of considerable evidence to the contrary. At Angel's party they danced together, drank plastic cupfuls of cheap red wine, and snogged sweatily in the corner. Alex pushed her down on a pile of coats, put one hand under her bra, and with the other guided her perfectly manicured fingers down to the tangled bulge at his crotch. He moaned, and Shireen turned her face away, faintly disgusted.

Eventually they left together and spent a steamy half hour in Alex's car, during which Shireen provided the requisite sexual satisfaction. Her new boyfriend did not return the favor, a fact she might have resented had she given it much thought.

In any case, the pairing stuck. From that evening, Shireen and Alex attended class together, ate lunch together, and did homework together. They only avoided full sexual intercourse together due to Shireen's squeamishness about bodily fluids and Alex's squeamishness about condoms.

Everyone at school knew about their attachment and felt cheered, secure in the knowledge that all things find their proper level; that the world is run by strict, transparent rules, and that elegant constructions rule romance as well as nature.

The information reached Justin, who feigned indifference.

Inwardly, however, he felt depressed by his growing collection of missed opportunities. The fact that he wasn't particularly interested in Shireen didn't interfere with the sense that he had failed to grasp the potential of their fledgling relationship. Not only was he a failure as a possible boyfriend, but his fate had expanded to include indifference and insignificant failures piling up inch by miserable inch to create an Everest of wasted effort, a teetering peak from which he would eventually fall to his death.

Agnes seemed to have forgotten he existed, or at least that was how he interpreted her silence. Ten times a day he sat immobilized in front of the telephone, rehearsing casual conversations with her in his head. For the first few days, Boy had watched intently, curious and encouraging. But even he gave up when it became obvious that Justin could not bring himself to act.

He took to his bed, told his mother it was flu, and stayed there for days, tossing in a fever of self-doubt. His mother knocked tentatively on his door each morning, felt his head, and pronounced him "not quite so warm as last time."

Not warm at all, he thought. Frigid, in fact.

The ring ring ring of the telephone disturbed his dreams. Eventually he answered it.

"What's happened to you?" Agnes was irate. "You've dropped off the face of the earth. What did you think of the pictures?"

"What pictures?"

What pictures? Agnes shook her head. He was some cool character, that Justin Case. "Never mind. When can we meet?"

"I'm not well."

She snorted. "You don't sound ill. You sound depressed. When was the last time you went out?"

He could hear her frown. "I went running a few days ago."

"*Aside* from running. School, the shops, a film, a friend. Anything."

He didn't answer.

"*Think*."

"A week or so?"

She hadn't seen him in two. "You're agoraphobic now, are you?"

"No," he said, annoyed. "I just don't feel like going out."

"Justin, no one except little old ladies with hundreds of cats stays home for a whole week. It's not normal. What are you doing now?"

"Nothing."

Agnes sighed. "I'll come get you," she said, and hung up.

When he answered the door his appearance shocked her. He'd lost weight and his skin looked faintly grayish. He wore rumpled sweats and his hair was long and greasy.

"Yuck," she said, "you look disgusting."

"Thank you."

His mother emerged from the kitchen with Charlie. She introduced herself to Agnes, holding out her hand with a diffident smile. "How nice to meet you."

Agnes studied her face for a clue to Justin's pathology. He didn't exactly look like his mother, but then, it was hard to find the resemblance when one person was so striking and the other so middle-aged. Like most people's parents, she looked worn and a little shapeless, her lips the same color as her skin, her hair beige and feathered into layers. From the creases around her eyes, Agnes guessed she was in her mid-forties. And there was definitely something of Justin in her expression after all. Something hesitant, off-balance.

Agnes followed Justin upstairs to his bedroom, where a boom box screamed out noise with a massively overbalanced bass line. Agnes wondered how anyone could live in such a pit of a room. It stank of male hormones and misery. She threw open a window, stood for a moment to inhale the cold clean air, then sat on the bed and looked him over.

"Don't you think you're taking this doomed youth thing a little too seriously?"

"Try living it."

"There's a fine line, you know. Between looking romantically shabby and just looking horrible."

Justin's eyes narrowed with anger. "I'm *not* interested in your fine line, and it's *not* romantic. And you may as well leave because I'm *not* going anywhere."

"Don't be snippy, it doesn't suit you." She took his arm and flashed her most beatific smile. "Come on, some air will do you good."

She waited for his resistance to dissolve, then tugged gently on his elbow. He dragged his feet like a child as she steered him down the stairs to the front hall, where his gray coat lay on a chair by the door. Agnes picked it up and handed it to him.

When she opened the door he hesitated, turning to look behind him.

She sighed. "Leave the dog. Let's go."

But the walk was not a success. Despite the crisp autumn day and a bright blue sky, Agnes's voice gave him a headache, and his legs felt tired and heavy. When at last they reached home, he said goodbye without raising the subject of another meeting, went straight to his room, and lay down. When his mother knocked, offering dinner, he pretended to be asleep.

He dozed, waking long after midnight to the sound of a regular thudding noise coming from his brother's room. After a few minutes, he slipped down the hall to investigate.

Peering around the door, he saw that Charlie was wide awake and studying a picture book. Across the room, a large, untidy heap of books had been flung from the crib.

At the sight of his brother, Charlie squeaked with delight. Face alight, he stood up and held out his arms. Justin switched on a lamp in the shape of a toy boat and swung the child up and out of his padded prison. Justin plunked him down on the floor, where he sat in his stretchy sleep suit, wearing an expression of intense concentration.

"Blocks," he said, pointing a chubby hand in the direction of the toy box.

Justin rummaged through the soft toys, musical instruments, games, sweets, and lost socks, tossing out as many of the painted wooden alphabet blocks as he could find.

"Do you want to make words?" Justin asked, pleased with his own altruism. Poor linguistically challenged little sod. Maybe he could teach him to swear.

His brother busied himself with the blocks.

J, S, T. He fixed Justin with an intent look.

Justin shook his head. "That doesn't spell anything," he said, reaching to find a vowel. "Look, C-A-T, cat."

The child sighed and snatched the blocks back, adding more letters to the ones on the floor.

J, S, T, N, C, A, S. There was a shortage of vowels.

Justin's attention wandered. He was already bored with this game. The child added an "E" to the end, and clapped his hands. "Look."

"Yes, fine, OK." Justin drifted back into humoring mode. "Hooray, well done, excellent. What have you spelled?"

He glanced at the letters, looked again, and froze. The blood drained from his face, and he stared at his brother. "Jesus Christ, how on earth did you do that?"

The child, busy with his task, didn't look up.

H, A, T.

Justin stared. "Justin Case hat? What? What are you trying to write?"

With a look of infinite patience, Charlie began to adjust the letters. "Look," he said again, with satisfaction.

Justin looked. The letters had been divided more carefully now, leaving large spaces between words so there could be no doubt as to the meaning.

JST IN CASE WHAT.

He looked at Charlie, then down again at the words.

Just in case what?

Just in case something irreversible occurs. *Just in case* he was maimed, injured, died. *Just in case* something so horrible happened to him, or to someone he knew, that he would never, ever recover.

Was it possible that the child understood the meaning of his own question? Could he have arranged the letters as a premeditated act? Or was it like monkeys at typewriters and eventually, if left here with an infinite supply of blocks, Charlie would fill the room with *Hamlet*?

The sheer cosmic strangeness of his brother's feat and the unlikely question in the cryptogram made Justin tremble. I must ask him, he thought, I must find a way to communicate with him. He fumbled for more blocks but it was too late. The child was fast asleep, fat pink fingers wrapped around the leg of his sock monkey.

Justin replaced him carefully in his crib, tucked a blanket under him, and slowly returned to his own bed. There he lay, spooked: a spinning pin in a celestial bowling alley.

Perhaps I could offer fate a truce, he thought. A deal. You live your life, I'll live mine. No surprises, no one gets hurt.

He fell asleep at dawn.

19

I DON'T MAKE DEALS, Justin. I deal.

And here's how your cards are falling: A couple of negligible hearts. A joker. A sad little club.

Will you draw?

Oh look! The ace of spades.

I *am* sorry.

20

JUSTIN AWOKE AT NOON with a start. He knew instantly and with utter certainty that he had to leave home. Fate was closing in, sending ominous messages in strange guises.

Just in case what? Oh ha ha. Why don't you talk to *me* instead of channeling evil questions through Charlie as if he were some sort of human Ouija board?

Just in case what?

Even in the bright light of day, the only response he could think of came in the form of a thousand hellish possibilities. But it didn't matter. He knew what he had to do. Packing a bag with a change of clothes and a toothbrush, he cracked open the door to his room and stepped out, ready to begin his journey.

Hello, said Charlie from the floor at his feet. One fat hand gripped his toy monkey, the other guided a large wooden spoon through the air like an airplane.

Justin lowered himself to the ground and looked his brother in the eye. "What was that business in the night?" he asked gently. "Since when have you learned to spell?"

Charlie held his brother's gaze for a moment before answering.

It was an important question I asked you in the night, he said, and you need to answer it or you'll never get over that time I tried to fly.

"Blocks!" he said emphatically, hitting the floor with his spoon.

Having expected no further explanation, Justin kissed the child, tucked his passport into his pocket, called his dog, told his mother his school trip had been moved forward a week, and set out for Luton Airport.

As he stepped onto the local bus, Justin felt the gravitational tug of his past loosening. It was a good feeling. The open road beckoned. The closer he came to the airport, the freer he felt, like a comet streaming off into a weightless infinity of possible encounters.

Main terminal, his stop. The *whoosh* of automatic airport doors and the great expanses of steel and glass excited him. There were no curtains, no occasional tables, no kitchen utensils. No heaps of dirty laundry or drawers filled with tartan pajamas. There was no letterbox. No milk on the doorstep. Nothing domestic, cozy, or familiar; nothing with his scent or his name or his National Insurance number on it.

Why hadn't he realized it before? The problem was all around him. The stuffy little room. The conventional parents, the dismal house. The street. The school. Here, all the little threads that connected him to earth could be broken. He was in transit, on the lam. He was Gulliver, Neil Armstrong, Bonnie and Clyde, all rolled into one.

Making his way to the information desk, Justin obtained an application allowing an unaccompanied minor to travel abroad, forged his parents' signatures, bought a sandwich and a coffee, and settled in to wait for a flight. One by one he considered destinations. Verona, Antalya. Rhodes, Zákinthos, Barcelona. Salzburg, Thessaloníki. Istanbul. Nîmes, Brest. Halifax.

For three hours he sat very still at the center of the airport, motionless like the human eye of a storm, until all the swirling activity blurred and made him sleepy. Moving to a quiet corner by the observation window, he folded his coat into a pillow, went to sleep, and dreamt he was a mouse in a maze. Round and round he ran until he found the pathway leading to freedom—blocked by the face of an enormous mechanical cat.

YEOWWWWW!

He leapt in his sleep, startled and disorientated, banging his head on the metal window frame. Boy was awake, watching him anxiously. But despite the terrifying image, Justin felt calm. The cat in his dream was a murderer, but the mouse was still alive.

He stretched, found the toilet. More hours passed, during which he drifted from kiosk to café, reading magazines dedicated to subjects that had never before interested him, flipping through foreign guidebooks, shaking plastic blizzards, observing the wax and wane of the shifting crowds. Time slipped past easily here. He felt inconspicuous, relaxed.

The next time hunger beckoned he sought out the Traveler's Café, pushed his tray around the chrome track with the rest of the In Transits, chose sausage and mash and peas, chocolate cake and orange juice, and paid for it with the pocket money for his school trip. He ate slowly, happy to be an observer. He was the only one with no mission, no plane to catch, no breakfast to serve, no children to entertain. All around milled anxious groups of travelers, all nationalities and all colors, all sizes and shapes and sexual persuasions.

Sometimes they smiled at him, struck by his face, his coat, or even his dog, establishing the most fleeting of human connections, a millisecond of brotherhood. We're all in this together, they said to him silently, in a hundred different languages.

And then, in a sudden blinding flash, he realized he no longer needed to comb the world in search of a destination.

He had arrived.

21

EIGHT HOURS spent stretched out along an undulating row of plastic seats is not everyone's idea of a good night's sleep. But with legs slotted under metal armrests, ten thousand watts of fluorescent light glaring directly overhead, hundreds of disgruntled travelers for company, an abandoned acrylic airline blanket for a cover, and his loyal dog at his feet, Justin slept like a baby.

He felt almost serene.

The rattle of the cleaner's trolley lulled him into the gentlest unconsciousness he had experienced in years. The intense artificial light gave him a powerful sense of well-being; it occurred to him that he'd spent most of his life afraid of the dark.

He slept through the early-morning arrivals and departures, waking refreshed and cheerful at 8 a.m.

The first day of his new life began with a full English breakfast at the café across from the first-class lounge. Except for the mushrooms, which tasted strongly of plastic, the meal was adequate: microwave hot and plentiful. When he asked for more toast, the middle-aged woman behind the counter waved his money away.

"You save that money for your journey," she said, handing him a plate heaped with slices of cold, singed white toast, a handful of individually wrapped butter pats, and five tiny tubs of strawberry jam.

He smiled at her.

Working his way through the pile of toast, Justin felt there was no pressure to do anything. His pace slowed accordingly, and it was nearly ten by the time he'd finished his food and read all the newspapers abandoned on surrounding tables.

He wiped his mouth and stacked his rubbish for the cleaners, left Boy to look after his belongings, followed the picture signs to the Comfort Zone, pushed a pound into the slot of a tall turnstile, entered the cubicle, stripped off his clothes, and stepped gratefully into the steamy blast of the airport shower. The thick stream of hot water felt like a miracle; he stood under it motionless, letting it pour through his hair, down his neck and back, over the narrow smooth planes of his hips, down his legs and off his ankles, swirling around the soles of his feet before disappearing down the plug hole. For ten minutes he stood, allowing the warmth to penetrate his muscles and soak through to his bones. It brought with it a realization of how lucky he was, how privileged to be alive and well and living at Luton Airport.

He spent so long in the steamy cubicle that the attendant had to bang on the door to move him along, but he didn't care. He felt peaceful, warmed through to the very core of his being. He turned off the water and at first the silence confused him. It was ages before he realized that the soundtrack that had accompanied his recent life—the constant buzzing white noise of anxiety—was gone.

He felt like singing, crying, shouting with relief.

He stared hard at himself in the mirror as he brushed his teeth, noticing that the face that stared back at him looked different. The haunted expression was gone. He looked less like a nervous child, more like a person.

The attendant pounded on the door, more loudly this time.

Justin dried his neck and ruffled his damp hair with a tear-off paper towel. He felt cleaner than he'd felt in his entire life. A pound's worth of soap and hot water was all it took to cleanse the grime from his soul, remove the sludge from his brain and reveal the face behind the mask.

He held his hand out in front of him. No trace of a tremor.

He was strong. Invincible.

Bring on your worst, he said to fate.

Indeed.

22

FOR THREE DAYS Justin lived in a state of suspended animation that passed for a sort of domestic bliss.

Each night he tucked himself into his molded plastic row of blue seats and slept deeply, his dog by his side. After the first night he dreamt a new dream. In this dream he was naked, submerged in air so thick and warm it buoyed him up, let him float like a zeppelin through the fuggy atmosphere of the airport. From his vantage point near the ceiling, he could observe the comings and goings of humanity like some lesser god, occasionally lowering his imaginary flaps to swoop among the people, amused, all-powerful, and playful.

Each morning he awoke loose-limbed, clearheaded, and optimistic.

He suddenly realized that what he felt was happy, and the feeling was so dramatically new, so different, he had to tell Agnes.

"Where are you?" she squawked down the phone. "I've been so worried."

"Luton Airport."

"Luton Airport?"

"Yes."

"Are you coming or going?"

"Just . . . staying."

"How strange." She was quiet for a moment. "Is it nice?"

"Yes. Perfect."

"Perfect? How, perfect?"

"Just perfect. I can't explain."

"Try."

He paused. "It's peaceful here. Nothing's familiar. No one knows who I am."

At the other end of the phone, she said nothing.

"It's not even a place, it's like a place on the way to another place. Like limbo."

"I never thought of it that way."

"Neither did I. But . . . there you are."

"There *you* are," she said, and he could hear the expression on her face.

Neither of them said anything. Then he heard the pips of his money running out.

"Agnes—"

"I'll be there in half an hour."

The phone went dead.

23

HE KNEW WITHIN SECONDS that she had arrived. Beside him, Boy flicked his ears back and forth and arranged himself along her line of approach. Even across the huge expanse of airport terminal, Justin recognized the strange pockets of quiet followed by a kind of murmuring buzz. He wondered what she was wearing.

From his elevated position on the observation deck, he could look down on nearly the whole space, and with affection and awe he observed the disturbed waves of crowd movement that described her path across the floor.

He could see her now, in her green snakeskin boots, heavy magenta tights, tiny green velour shorts, and a stretchy, nearly transparent shirt with sleeves that extended past the ends of her fingertips almost to the floor. Under one arm she carried the huge shaggy pelt of an enormous acrylic beast. A pointy white woolen hat with bright bobbing pom-poms covered the crown of her pink head; her camera bag completed the outfit.

Now he could hear her too, even from up here, the clomp clomp clomp of the thick-soled boots.

He smiled, and for a moment felt deeply touched by her friendship. He leaned over the balcony and waved to her.

"Agnes!" he called. She looked up and beamed at him, managing to click off a few shots on a long lens while waving excitedly.

He pointed to the escalator at the far end of the terminal, and, arriving almost the same moment she did, started down towards her. Boy stood at the top, shivering and whining. He gave a long howling bark, the first Justin had ever heard from him.

But he had no time to think about Boy.

Too impatient to wait, Agnes had stepped onto the up escalator. As they converged, traveling in opposite directions, she hiked herself up over the moving handrail, climbed awkwardly across the center section, and dropped onto the step below his with a great *clump*. She stepped back and appraised him.

"You look different," she said, frowning, as she changed lenses on her camera. "Better."

He nodded.

"What about"—she lowered her voice—"you know?"

He spread his hands and shrugged, but the words tumbled

out. "Something has changed. I feel lighter, happier. Free. Like a weight has lifted. I know it sounds ridiculously melodramatic"—he grinned, unable to suppress the feeling of joy—"but he's *gone*."

The two inclined their bodies slightly forwards, whether to kiss or simply to step together off the bottom of the escalator is impossible to know. For in the split second that followed, the air was rent by an explosion so loud, they felt its vibration penetrate the soft tissues of their bodies before they heard it, felt it hurl them two meters or more into the air and smash them back violently to the ground, along with every other person in the airport, even the ones who were dead.

24

ASK ANY COMEDIAN, tennis player, chef. Timing is everything.

25

WHO KNOWS what to expect from a blast of that magnitude? The brain struggles to process information with which it has no experience, races to find an explanation for the searing pain in one shoulder, the awkward bend of a leg folded under and digging into your solar plexus, a leg that turns out not to be your own.

At first everything seems utterly quiet, except for a continuous tintinnabulation, like church bells.

Then as your eyes adjust to the singular angle of your head, and you manage to lift it enough to look around you, it becomes obvious that what you are experiencing isn't silence at all, rather an extreme, blast-induced inability to hear. All around are events signaling noise, mouths open in the posture of screams.

Huge panes of glass splinter from within bent window frames, crashing much too slowly and silently to the ground.

You suddenly remember another person, her name escapes you but you know what she looks like and you know she isn't there, or at least that you can't see her within the forty-five degrees of your vision. You haul yourself slowly, painfully, up onto your knees and look around, calmly, for calamity is, after all, what you've been expecting all along, and what you see that appears to have caused all this commotion is the nose of an enormous airplane, crushed and smoking, arranged almost perfectly perpendicular to the floor of approximately the place where you were standing five minutes ago. The plane is nearly intact, balanced unnaturally on its head like a monstrous gray pachyderm in a grotesque three-ring circus. Your eyes follow it upwards, mesmerized by the slight sway of the fuselage, or at least that part of it not obscured from sight by what remains of the terminal roof.

This is even worse than you expected. But you have to admit, in some small way, it is gratifying.

I told you so.

I told you so.

People are beginning to stir now, and now is when you notice the pretty tongues of flame, fascinatingly orange, delicate and polite, gliding softly over the surface of the plane.

There is a hand on your shoulder, the one that hurts, and the girl whose name you can't remember is standing next to you. Swaying, more than standing. Her face is bloody but she doesn't appear to be in pain. She holds a camera in one hand and tries to say something to you but you just stare at her and smile, because you are quite happy to see her. You see her mouth move with words addressed to you, though you can hear nothing at all.

She takes your hand, pulls you to your feet, and the two of you begin to walk, unsteadily because of all the debris and the bodies and the parts of bodies in your way, not to mention the bruises and as yet uncataloged injuries spread across your own bodies, and a certain unsteadiness caused by shock. You begin walking faster, almost jogging once you get a little better at avoiding things that you remember could be dangerous, or disgusting, and also you remember how to move quickly, which was never something you imagined you could forget, even for a few minutes. You are starting to remember lots of things, like about fire, and how it can be dangerous and harmful, as you jog towards a hole that has been blasted through the side of the building, picking your way as carefully as possible over the inert bodies of the injured and dead, avoiding molten drips of metal, lethal tottering icicles of glass, pools of blood.

Some of the things you see are curious and might have been disturbing in another context where they seemed more real. One person's legs look all wrong as if they're on backwards and there's a hand on the floor all on its own looking somehow careless. A little further away there's what looks like a torso with no arms and you're glad for a minute that you can't hear any of the noises coming from the torso's head.

Then you stop and look down and see one of the strangest things you have seen yet that day. It is an oversized magazine on the ground, creased open and spattered with blood. There is a picture of a boy in the magazine and he is wearing clothes that look vaguely familiar; there is something in the face staring up at you that reminds you of someone or something.

The boy in the pictures is slim and stands with his body partially turned away from you. His hair is longish, his skin very pale. He has his hands crammed into the front pockets of his jeans. The expression on his face is slightly blurred.

There is a large caption on the top of the page but some of it has been smeared with blood. The bit you can still make out reads: DOOMED YOUTH.

You are not allowed to stop and think about this strange picture, for in no time at all you are being pulled forwards and then you are outside, breathing air that doesn't hurt your lungs like the acrid heavy air in the terminal.

It is a relief to be outside, away from the silent screaming mouths and all the falling rubble. When she's not taking pictures, the girl keeps pulling at your arm, which is starting to annoy you and feels painful, but her grip is surprisingly strong given how small and delicate she looks and the fact that she is barefoot, and you can tell from the bloody footprints she leaves that the bottoms of her feet are bleeding.

You want to stop and look around, wish you had your own camera to take some pictures of the astonishing sight of a substantially intact DC-10 standing on its nose in the center of your new home. But you give in to the pressure on your arm because fighting it just causes it to hurt more, and the last thing you require just now is more pain. You are nearly crying with the pain by the time she lets you stop and turn around, and nudges you to follow the direction of the finger she points at the part of the plane now swallowed in flame, and then succumbing once more to the pressure of her hand on yours, you begin to move and as your feet hit the tarmac in the nice familiar rhythm of running, the words that go through your head sweetly and deliciously like a kind of nursery rhyme gone wrong are doomed youth doomed youth doomed youth.

26

DON'T GET SNIFFY with me. I get no particular pleasure out of tragedy.

Some days nothing but good deeds will do.

Who do you think brings lovers together, reunites long-lost siblings, effects miracle cures? Who makes cripples dance, half-wits think?

Survivors survive.

27

"IT'S OK, Justin, I think we can stop now."

Agnes was speaking loudly, just an inch or two from his ear, but he didn't flinch, or react, or turn around, or give any indication that he'd heard. She tapped him, and when he turned from the mesmerizing sight of the burning terminal, she pressed her hands palms down towards the ground, the way a nursery teacher calms and settles children in a classroom and tells them it is time to sit.

Justin sat.

They were far enough away to be safe now; even an explosion would have to cross the four main north-south runways to get to them. She was panting and for the first time felt the pain in her feet, cut as they crossed the terminal floor. Her head was clear and the sequence of events transparent enough for her to wonder how her shoes had come off and when. It seemed such an odd consequence of a blast.

As they sat, a small fireball rolled up the tail of the DC-10, then another, and another, then the black smoke pouring out of the smashed nose thickened, and finally they saw, then heard, the explosion that ripped the plane to pieces and destroyed what was left of the terminal.

Justin stared like a bush baby, his eyes huge, unblinking and seemingly disconnected from his brain. He looked more like a child than the disorientated teenager he was, a child watching fireworks, excited, waiting for the next explosion.

Well, you had to give the boy credit, Agnes thought. He'd sure hit the nail on the head with his crazy doom stuff. Not that she thought he'd been making it up exactly, but doom had always seemed a somewhat melodramatic expression of what she took to be ordinary teenage anxiety. She wondered if he could have known about this all along, whether the plane crash had somehow been wired in as a premonition of his fate.

It hurt her head to think so hard about something so difficult to grasp.

She wondered, as she sat bleeding slowly, watching what remained of the terminal melt into a soup of glass and metal and human flesh on the ground, if they were alive because of being blessed or in spite of being cursed.

She wondered if this was the end or the beginning of Justin's clash with fate.

Or just some fairly average incident in the middle.

28

THE CRASH made front-page news as far away as Los Angeles and Beijing, providing press coverage for international terror pundits the world over. Scotland Yard stepped in and a massive police hunt was launched, suspects arrested, video footage examined over and over for clues.

It would be months before investigators finally filed a report citing the age of the plane and mechanical failure for the tragedy. Much to the disappointment of the press, no evidence of terrorism, conspiracy, or foul play emerged.

But Justin didn't need the report. He knew who was responsible.

It took a great deal of self-control to overcome his impulse to confess to crash investigators. If the bullet meant for you kills an innocent bystander do you become an accessory to murder?

He went home with Agnes. "Just for a day or two," he begged.

And how could she refuse? He was obviously in shock and besides, would have a great deal of explaining to do. His parents thought he was on a class trip. In Wales.

They arrived at her flat, shutting the door against the world like refugees. The familiar objects, the smell, the color and warmth of home calmed Agnes, but Justin's leg jiggled and the twitch in his left eye intensified. He ran his fingertips repeatedly back and forth over the short soft nap of a velvet chair while she made up the sofa with clean sheets. She rummaged in a drawer for pajamas that would fit him, then collapsed into bed herself, exhausted.

At 4 a.m. she woke with a start, heart pounding, to a scratching noise at the bedroom door, like an animal.

It was Justin, fully dressed, wild-eyed and trying to smile.

"Meow," he said. "You need a cat flap."

Agnes slumped back against the pillows. "What is it, Justin, can't you sleep?" He shook his head and she stumbled out of bed with a sigh.

"I'll make a cup of tea."

She returned with a tray and Justin watched the fingers of her left hand as she poured milk into steaming cups. He felt awkward and unconnected to the world of people. I'd like to have sex with her fingers, he thought, squeezing his eyes shut.

When he opened them again she had reached for her camera.

"Agnes . . . ," he began.

"Yes, Justin?" Click click click.

"Agnes, *please*. My dog is missing."

Agnes lowered the camera as he leapt to his feet and began pacing, his face crumpled with misery.

"I haven't seen him since the plane crash."

"Justin, come and sit down. I'm sorry about your dog."

He glared at her. "No you're not. You're humoring me."

She flared back. "Well, I *am* sorry about your dog. I'm sorry he exists in the first place."

Justin looked as if she'd slapped him.

She turned away. "Please, Justin. This isn't easy for me, either."

He sat down, leg jiggling nervously, angrily.

"I saw something at the airport, Agnes."

Despite the horror, she was desperate to sort through her photographs and review the disaster close up. She wondered what particular detail amid the devastation had spooked him.

"Why didn't you show me?"

"Show you what, Justin?"

"The magazine. *Doomed Youth*."

She was taken aback. "I *did* show you. I gave it to you as soon as it came out. I asked you how you liked it."

He tried to think, but his brain wouldn't organize the thoughts. Agitated, he shook his head. "It doesn't matter. Don't you see what you did? You jinxed me. It's your fault. I didn't need to be any more doomed than I was already."

"Justin—"

"What?"

"You looked beautiful."

"I looked doomed."

Agnes felt unnerved. She couldn't keep up with his train of thought. "Justin, can't you sit down, please? Haven't you slept at all?"

"The sleep of the dead. The damned. In answer to your question, no." He turned to face her once more, eyes glinting and full of sorrow. "How can I sleep with a conscience full of blood?"

He swiped his face with the back of his hand and she saw that he was exhausted, and scared.

"Justin, you don't feel responsible, do you?"

He spun off around the room. "Of course I don't. Of course I do."

Agnes got up, took hold of his arm, and pushed him gently back onto the sofa.

"I was right, Agnes, wasn't I right?"

"Please, Justin. Can't you stop for a moment? You're confused."

"No I'm not." He smiled an awful smile. "I'm clearer than I've ever been. I can *see* things."

Agnes felt a jab of fear. "What things?"

"Things that might happen. Illness, death, catastrophe." He lapsed into a grotesque cowboy accent. "*Stay away from me baby, I'm trouble.*"

Agnes spoke to him slowly, calmly. "Justin? You're alive. You're OK now. It's over."

"No." His expression was fierce.

Then he stood up, grabbed a copy of the oversized magazine

from a neat pile by the sofa, and slammed it down on the table. He didn't even have to search. It fell open to his picture under the headline ANTHEM FOR DOOMED YOUTH. He stared out at himself with a face anticipating catastrophe.

"It's just fashion, Justin."

"*Really?* It looks more like bloody *Nostradamus* to me."

Oh boy, Agnes thought as he stormed out, slamming the door behind him. He's at least right about one thing.

It's not over. Not yet.

29

IN THE AFTERMATH of the crash, Agnes spent most of her waking hours at her studio. It was a refuge, and she found it impossible to look away from the downloaded images flashing up on her computer screen. She sold a handful of photos to a news agency, one of which showed the blurred figure of a boy in a distinctive gray leather coat in the background. The best ones she saved for herself.

Left alone, Justin braved the rain and cold at all hours of day and night, combing the neighborhood for Boy. He rang Agnes from every phone box he passed, spouting incoherent cosmic conspiracy theories until she stopped answering. Then he left messages.

"I've notified all the dog shelters, the police, the army," he told the answerphone in a voice ragged with anguish. "If I had a photo I could put posters up, but it won't do any good if he's been murdered. Do you think he's been murdered? *Agnes? Are you there? Pick up the phone!*" Then he set off again, whistling for Boy. His feet splashed across uneven tarmac, through oily puddles, the monotonous sameness of suburban sprawl distracting him not at all from the buzzing panic in his brain.

Agnes tried telling herself he would come to terms with the tragedy, would return, with time, to something like normal. If only he would go home, go back to school, forget about his stupid dog. Especially that.

When she put her key in the door, she did it silently, hoping he'd be asleep. We can't go on like this, she thought, slipping into bed, relieved and guilty at his absence. He's a mess. He needs help. I'll go mad.

She was fast asleep by the time he returned. Out of consideration, he knocked softly. Then leaned on the bell.

She came eventually, wrapped in a short silk robe. Even straight out of bed her hair lay glossy and smooth against her head. He wanted to touch it. She looked regal, like a Japanese princess.

"Come in, Justin." She yawned.

"I can't find him."

"I gathered that. You're soaked. Have you eaten anything today?"

Justin shook his head and looked at the clock. Four forty-one. No wonder it was so dark.

She fetched him a towel. "I'll put some clothes on. The café opens at five."

Agnes led him down the street. It was cold, and his coat was sodden. They entered the little café and she greeted the waitress. The place was already crowded with people on their way home from clubs; it smelled of sausage and beans and grease and sweat. The windows were opaque with steam. They squeezed into a cramped booth in the corner, and Agnes ordered tea and full English breakfast for them both. She hung his wet coat on a hook and gave him her scarf, which he wrapped around his neck and shoulders, grateful for the warmth.

"I don't need to ask how you are," she said. "I can see for myself."

He sipped his tea, hands curled round the mug, face buried in the steam.

"You haven't talked to anyone today?"

"Only you."

"Have you phoned your parents? What about school? Have you told anyone at all?"

He shook his head.

Their breakfast arrived, and he pushed the beans around his plate with a knife.

"Maybe you should see a doctor."

"Fate is trying to kill me. I miss my dog. What's a doctor going to say? You're not ill, you're mad as a muffin? They'll either lock me up or tell me to get a grip and no one will believe the truth anyway."

"What exactly is the truth?"

He said nothing.

"Justin?" Agnes sighed, taking his hand and speaking to him gently. "It *is* horrible. I can't stop thinking about all the blood, seeing it, and the screaming people. I can't stand loud noises, they make me jump out of my skin. I'm terrified of crowds. But *I don't feel responsible*. We just happened to be there, along with a thousand other people."

"That's your truth. Mine's different." He pulled his hand back and immediately wished he hadn't. "At least you were there, Agnes. At least you saw it happen, you know I didn't imagine it. The plane landed exactly where I was standing three minutes earlier. I didn't imagine that, did I?" His voice was pleading.

"No, you didn't. It's just hard for me to think of it as—" She paused. "As anything other than a monstrous coincidence."

Justin scanned her face, desperate to define the experience in a way that included them both. "Maybe it doesn't make any difference how you think of it."

"Oh, Justin." She looked back at him, defeated. "Don't you see? It makes all the difference in the world."

She called for the bill, paid it, and they walked home together in the gray dawn. Agnes stopped at the front door to pull off her shoes. By the time she entered the flat, he was lying curled up on her bed, asleep.

She covered him with a blanket.

A few hours later, Justin stirred. He blinked open his eyes, and found Agnes sitting next to him.

She looked down, her face kind. "Hello."

Her voice sent a thousand volts of electricity through him, turned him one-dimensional with need.

"Are you feeling any better?"

He couldn't think and he couldn't help himself. He reached up and kissed her, kissed her so unself-consciously and with so much purity of intent that she put her better instincts on hold and kissed him back.

This is the way the world ends . . .

She felt generous, relieved, excited by the intensity of his desire. *I am helping him,* she lied.

He didn't unbutton her top, just slipped his hands underneath to the warm space next to her skin, pressing his mouth to her face and her neck, so that by the time she reconsidered, remembered that this was Justin, mad Justin dancing on the head of a pin like a deranged angel, by that time it was too late, and it no longer mattered much who he was.

This is the way the world ends . . .

There was another explosion, this time inside his brain. Afterwards he felt calm, for the first time since the crash. The love overflowed his body and filled the room.

He's very nice like this, Agnes thought.

Instead of falling asleep, he stared and stared at her as if she were all he required till the end of time.

It was flattering to be stared at that way.

And then he buried his head in her arms and cried, told her how amazing she was, how kind, how generous, how wise. He clung to her as the oxygen in the room grew thin, depleted by too many intakes of breath, too many outpourings of love. She needed to get up, run away, escape his overpowering need and the knowledge that she had done something she wished she hadn't.

This is the way the world ends . . .

It was the sharp edge of charity that compelled her to stay until he fell asleep again, after which she crept out of bed, showered, left him a note, and with a mingled feeling of relief and guilt, shut the door behind her and went out.

Not with a bang but a whimper.

30

AGNES PHONED his parents. She had promised not to tell them about his presence at the airport, but in her opinion, he needed help. Or more to the point, she did. She hoped they would come get him or at least suggest an alternate solution to what Agnes felt wasn't entirely her problem.

His mother, however, merely thanked Agnes for allowing him to stay. "You're terribly kind to have him. We really don't know what to do. Before he went to Wales he just drifted around the house like a ghost."

Agnes stared at the phone.

"His father and I keep hoping he'll grow out of it."

Agnes shook her head in disbelief. Grow out of it? But how? He *is* it. "I think you should come see him."

"Yes," said his mother.

"Tomorrow."

Agnes put down the phone. Some people just shouldn't be parents, she thought. Like me, now.

Justin's mother arrived with Charlie as Agnes was going out. They met at the door.

"I'm sorry to run off," Agnes said. "Justin's still asleep. He was out late again, searching for *his dog*." She looked hard at the other woman, who fussed with her gloves.

His dog's gone missing? thought Charlie.

"I have to go, but make yourself at home." Agnes sighed. "There's tea and coffee in the kitchen."

While his mother hovered uncertainly, Charlie toddled over to the sofa where Justin lay sleeping, steadied himself against the edge, and leant in close.

Justin opened his eyes to find his brother's face just inches from his own.

"*Charlie?*"

What's happened to you? Charlie asked.

Justin propped himself up on one arm. His eyes burned. "I was right," he said, in a conspiratorial whisper. "A plane tried to land on me. Nobody believes me but *I was right*. And Boy's missing." His voice broke. "I think he's dead."

Charlie watched his brother's hands, fluttering and nervy, the fingers raw and bitten to the quick.

"David?"

Justin sat up as his mother kissed him awkwardly.

"How was Wales, darling?"

Wales? What Wales? Whales? Wails?

"How was the weather? Were the tents waterproof? Was the scenery nice? What about the food?"

He closed his eyes.

"There was a terrible plane crash while you were away." She shook her head. "Nowhere's safe these days."

He didn't respond and she accepted his silence, having lost her parental bearings so completely that she no longer knew what sort of behavior to expect from him.

"Perhaps, really, you should come home, darling. You don't look well."

Now there's a coincidence, he thought.

His mother turned away, face creased with worry. She found it difficult to accept that his behavior fit within the acceptable boundaries of teenage anxiety. But what could she do? She couldn't exactly order him to come home. His friend seemed nice enough, but was it right for a fifteen-year-old boy to be living with an older girl?

"Would you like some breakfast?"

He nodded, and she went off, relieved to postpone further conversation. In the kitchen she poured cereal and milk into a bowl, wondering when things had started to unravel. Perhaps she'd taken her eye off the ball when Charlie was born. Perhaps David was acting out of jealousy. She knew what the books had to say about sibling rivalry, but had hoped that, at nearly sixteen, he would be less susceptible.

How could she possibly know what was normal? Perhaps David was one of those boys who found adolescence uncomfortable. Perhaps he was merely going through a stage—a jabbering, incoherent, haunted, insomniac stage, from which he would emerge calm and self-possessed, pass his exams, get a job, meet a nice girl, buy a house, raise children, retire, have a heart attack, enjoy a good turnout at his funeral.

She placed the bowl by the sofa and took his hands in hers. "Wouldn't you like to come home, David?"

Justin stood up and left the room.

On the other hand, perhaps he could stay here, just for now. Perhaps he needs time away, a change of scene.

Or perhaps he's in love with Agnes. Suddenly it all made sense: the eccentric behavior, the mood swings, the nerves. First love, of course! Well. She certainly wasn't going to be one of those obstructive mothers, the ones who preached morality and abstinence at every turn. Let him have his love affair. She'd help him pick up the pieces when it ended.

Charlie gazed at his mother, unable to make sense of her expression. He padded around the flat after his brother, trying to talk to him. But Justin looked past him, and eventually retreated to the bathroom, where he locked the door. Charlie leant against it, defeated.

His mother tapped softly, but receiving no answer, called goodbye, reminded him to eat, and then—humming a little—packed Charlie into his stroller and left.

31

JUSTIN STAYED ON at Agnes's flat.

It was not so much a moving-in as a not-moving-out, and it wasn't at all what she'd had in mind. But he was only fifteen. He wasn't well. She felt guilty.

Justin didn't question his exile from Agnes's bed, but spent most of his time hunched on the sofa, watching her, his eyes tragic and dilated with love.

After living with his middle-of-the-night wanderings and insomnia, Agnes now had to check morning and evening that he hadn't fallen into a coma. He slept almost constantly and showed no real interest in food, though he would eat dutifully, like a child, any meal she put in front of him.

But she was not a cruel person (she told herself) and she

wasn't about to throw him out on the street. So it was with a large measure of resignation that she left for her studio each morning, leaving Justin fast asleep on the sofa.

After two or three days, she arrived to find him staring gloomily at *MasterChef* on TV. And she had an idea.

"Justin, I'm working so hard, and I haven't had a decent meal in days. What if I leave you some cash and a cookbook and you see what you can do?"

He looked shocked. What *can* I do? I can panic at the possibility of having to venture out of the flat. Or having to cook.

Why didn't she ask a question he knew the answer to, like would you like to have sex with me again?

But then he realized that this was something he could do for her that would make her life easier, a way to thank her for being kind to him. A way to win back her love. Yes, it would require getting dressed, going out, making choices, calculating change, following directions. But he owed her so much. It would be a start.

He told her he would try.

The next day, a Saturday, she left some money on the kitchen table with a copy of *Cooking World*, and went off to the studio.

He made it as far as the butcher on the corner. It was an old-fashioned family butcher, one of the few left in town, and there was a semiskinned rabbit hanging upside down in the window. Justin caught its eye and it winked at him. He recoiled in horror.

And then he heard the horrible whispery voice, only this time it was singing in a high-pitched, squeaky tone, like a rabbit's. When he dared look again, he saw that it was the rabbit singing, its dead mouth opening and closing with the words.

Run rabbit, run rabbit, run run run . . .

Where was his greyhound now, when he needed him? He tried ignoring the horrible figment of his imagination, hoping it would go away, but the rabbit continued to sing.

Bang! Bang! Bang! Goes the farmer's gun . . .

Justin forced himself to walk to the meat counter where the butcher stood chatting casually with a woman and her daughter, a soft-featured, sturdy girl with thick brown hair and clear, fearless eyes. All three seemed strangely impervious to the singing rabbit but when Justin approached, they turned to look at him.

He was a peculiar sight. Tears rolling down his face, shouting to drown out the rabbit's voice, he said he needed help, pointed to a chicken, handed over some money, grabbed his parcel, and bolted out the door.

Boys, thought the butcher.

Drugs, thought the woman.

Justin Case, thought Dorothea. So we meet again.

He heard the terrifying voice of the rabbit shouting after him.

SO RUN rabbit RUN rabbit run run RUN!

He ran, shaking with fear. He couldn't look at the chicken, its loose yellowy flesh reminded him too much of his own. It looked pathetic, naked and dead. He couldn't bear to touch it, began to cry when he thought how vulnerable chickens were, how misused, how short and tragic their lives.

He missed his brother. His dog. His former self.

When Agnes returned home, she found Justin curled up asleep in the fetal position and the chicken, still wrapped in paper, leaking blood into the burners of her stove.

Well, she thought, I wouldn't call the experiment an unqualified success.

She cleaned up the mess, rubbed the bird with salt and oil, stuffed it with a lemon, and placed it in a hot oven along with some ancient potatoes and beans from the bottom of the fridge.

An hour later the smell woke Justin, who, for a brief ecstatic moment, thought he'd managed to cook a meal by himself. Agnes would be impressed and grateful; she would invite him across the flat once more and into her bed. The reality disappointed but did not surprise him.

That night they ate together.

He didn't tell her about the singing rabbit, just sat and listened as she talked about her day, the photographs, her plan for a show. As the narrative unfurled he stopped hearing her words and listened instead to the delicious cadence of her speech. The sound of her voice soothed him; he drew it around his shoulders like fleece.

I will feed Agnes, he thought, and in exchange she will take me back.

And so he set about channeling every ounce of fear, anxiety, nervous energy, and love—especially love—into food.

The next morning he found a recipe for meatballs, uncrumpled the money left over from yesterday's chicken, shoved it into his pocket, and ventured out. The brightness of the day hurt his eyes, but the world felt cold and pleasant against his skin.

He approached the butcher's window cautiously. The rabbit was gone.

Perhaps he had imagined it.

He entered, asked the butcher for five hundred grams of ground beef, handed him the money, accepted his package and his change, and left.

As he passed the window again, he felt cautiously triumphant. He risked a tiny sideways glance. Still no rabbit. Excellent.

The way another person might have pursued the meaning of life, Justin made meatballs, shaping each ball into a sphere so labored and perfect it caused his eyes to fill with tears: for the flesh of the noble cow, for the perfection of three-dimensional geometric forms in nature, for the relentless universality of dinnertime.

He tried explaining this to Agnes and she laughed, but stopped when she caught sight of the expression on his face. He turned away before she could see the tears fall.

Oh lord, she thought. Woods. Not out of yet.

She hoped the cooking would bring him out of himself, lead him back into the real world.

But it didn't. In the kitchen he was like the sorcerer's apprentice: once he started, he couldn't stop. The orderly rhythm of recipes calmed his jangled nerves; there was no need for value judgments and approximations. He disliked pinches and handfuls, hungered after precise measures and medium (not small, not large) eggs. It calmed him to choose ingredients, to prepare each according to its true inner nature. The feel of raw materials and the sound of sizzling comforted him.

It comforted him most of all to feed Agnes.

"It's good, Justin, you're a natural," Agnes said, helping herself to another meatball.

Yes, he was a natural. A natural lunatic. But he enjoyed putting his mind to simple tasks, enjoyed her approval, enjoyed her pleasure at eating something other than sandwiches. It made him feel closer to the person he had been not so long ago, before his brain got all tied up in catastrophe.

And he felt closer, if only by teaspoons, to his heart's desire.

32

JUSTIN HAD PLANNED a special meal to celebrate two weeks of living with Agnes. As he adjusted the heat under the lamb steaks, he heard a knock on the door.

Wrapped in a thick winter coat, Peter Prince looked gawky and unfazed as ever, like a relic from a past life Justin had almost forgotten. Beside him stood his sister.

"Do you remember Dorothea?" Peter asked.

"Hello," she said, noting the dark circles under Justin's eyes.

Though her face looked familiar, Justin didn't recall having met her before.

The three stood in awkward silence. Justin wished they would go away. He squeezed his eyes shut, but when he opened them again, brother and sister were still there.

Peter smiled his awkward smile. "Your mother said you were living here now."

"Yes."

"Something smells good."

"Lamb."

During this exchange, Dorothea observed Justin. Justin, who had often marveled at Peter's ability to sustain an uncomfortably long silence, now wondered if the talent were genetic.

He sighed at last, defeated. "Won't you come in?"

Peter brightened. "Thanks. That would be nice." He stepped in before Justin could change his mind and, once inside, looked carefully around the little flat. He noted the crumpled duvet on the sofa, the breakfast dishes still on the table, the sink full of water and unwashed mugs. "You don't come to school anymore," he said.

Justin nodded.

"Or cross-country. Coach was asking what happened to you."

"Worried, was he?"

"I wouldn't say worried exactly. Hacked off, more like. I think your lamb is burning."

Justin dashed to the stove, grabbed the frying pan and hurled it onto the kitchen table. Having seared his palm on the handle, he reached over to turn the heat off with his good hand, plunging the other into the sinkful of dirty cold water. Smoke continued to billow from the burning frying pan. He stared at the charred meat as the smoke alarm began to shrill.

Peter grabbed a tea towel and fanned it violently under the

alarm, while an unruffled Dorothea walked over to the window and opened it.

Eventually the noise stopped and the smoke cleared.

"I saw a picture of the airport disaster," Peter said, in the dramatic quiet left by the shrieking alarm. "And—" He hesitated. "I thought I saw you."

Justin stared.

"My god, you are one lucky guy."

"Lucky?" Justin pronounced the word with exaggerated care, his teeth clenched, his entire body rigid with disbelief. Dorothea removed his burnt hand from the dirty sink water and examined it.

Peter blushed. "Uh . . . well, yes, lucky. The way I figure it, you must be just about the luckiest guy on earth."

"Are you *totally, utterly insane*? I've nearly been blown to smithereens in a freak airport accident, just about had a plane land in my lap. It's the first time in history anything bad has ever happened at Luton Airport and I just *happen* to be *inches from the epicenter*. The fact that I'm here is thanks only to the bizarre coincidence of Agnes arriving five minutes this side of apocalypse, thus saving me from spending the rest of my days as *a teaspoonful of vapor*."

Peter nodded sympathetically. "Yes, I guess so. Only . . ."

"Only *what?*"

"Only . . . you're still alive. She *did* arrive, and you weren't vaporized. And you did choose to live in an airport, which strikes me as kind of dangerous in the first place. Airports! I mean, think about it. They're a hub, a crossroads for all sorts of low-life operators: drug dealers, pickpockets, international criminals, forgers, arms dealers, black marketeers, smugglers, slave traders, spies, deposed dictators . . ."

As Peter totted up the potential horrors on the fingers of his left hand, Justin froze, though it might be more accurate to say that time ceased to advance around him. He experienced a kind of philosophical vertigo, his thoughts spinning wildly as Peter's words sank in.

One lucky guy.

His brother hadn't fallen out the window. He himself had survived a blast of epic proportions that should have killed him.

Maybe he was lucky after all.

He didn't feel lucky, but he *was* alive. Thanks to luck, and to Agnes. Without her, he had nothing. Without her, it was possible that he would cease to exist altogether.

Dorothea wrapped a clean tea towel around Justin's hand. "You'll live," she said calmly, and he stared at her.

Peter glanced around the flat once more. "Where's Boy?"

Justin sighed. "I don't know. I haven't seen him since the crash."

Peter looked genuinely shocked. "No wonder you're so upset."

And suddenly Justin remembered why he liked Peter, and was grateful.

They heard a key in the door. Agnes entered grumpily, stomping her feet and shaking the rain off her umbrella. "It's vile out there. Is something burning?" She spied Peter. "Oh, hello. You're the boy from the track team."

Peter's smile was shy. "Peter. It's nice to meet you. This is my sister, Dorothea. It's your supper that's burnt, I'm afraid. You look amazing."

She did. Her mac covered a tiny flutter of patterned skirt, pale green tights, and a skinny green turtleneck over which she wore a pink satin Edwardian corset. She sat down and removed her boots and a large green vinyl fireman's hat, shook the hat violently, and threw it on the back of the sofa. She was secretly pleased Peter and his sister had come, saving her from another tense evening with Justin.

"I could make cheese on toast," Peter offered. "It's my fault Justin burnt the meat."

Dorothea watched Agnes. She takes up a lot of space, Dorothea thought, like a particularly colorful parrot. And she wants him out, that's for sure.

Peter and Dorothea stayed for dinner. Agnes dug a pizza out of the freezer and scraped a salad together from what was left in the fridge. She poured herself a glass of wine, and as they ate, they talked about a new movie none of them had seen, the latest band from Norway, and endangered birds.

After they left, Justin slugged the dregs of the wine, attempted to kiss Agnes, accepted her cheek with furious self-loathing, and crawled like a cur into bed on the sofa.

On the way home, Dorothea thought about magnets, repelling as easily and naturally as they attract.

33

JUSTIN DIDN'T SLEEP that night. He lay awake thinking about luck.

When Agnes returned home the next evening, he had showered and dressed. He'd even made a stab at cutting his hair, though not a noticeably effective one. He had managed to tidy the flat, open the windows, put his sheets in the washing machine, fold all his things neatly and stow them in Agnes's wardrobe, set the table, and put out two wineglasses. He prepared a filet of pork in a peppercorn sauce that smelled delicious.

Instead of looking pleased, Agnes peered at him closely, unsmiling, her expression worried. "How are you, Justin?"

He spoke carefully. "I'm feeling a lot better, thank you."

She waited.

"Agnes?"

"Yes?"

"You know when Peter and Dorothea stopped by yesterday?"

"Yes?"

"Before you came home, we talked. I burnt the meat. Peter said they missed me at cross-country."

Agnes's smile was strained.

"He said"—Justin took a deep breath and closed his eyes—"he said I'm the luckiest person he knows."

Agnes burst out laughing. It was so unexpected. "What did you say in return?" she asked, picking up her camera.

"Put it *away*." He took a swing at it, furious. "I told him I *am* the luckiest person on earth. And it's all because of you." He paused. "I love you, Agnes."

"Thank you, Justin. I love you too."

"You do?" He beamed, picked up a carving knife, and began sawing thick slices of pork.

"Justin? What exactly are we talking about?"

"Love. I love you. I'm madly in love with you. Well, madly obviously, given I'm mad as a mudlark. But you saved my life. I'd be dead without you. And you're so good to me. And you love me too. How lucky is that? Amazing! Amazingly lucky. I can't live without you. You're my lucky charm."

She felt a sudden desire to kill Justin's well-meaning friend.

"I'm not your lucky charm, Justin—"

He interrupted. "Have some pork. Oh yes you are. You're my four-leaf clover. My rabbit's foot. My amulet. Without you I'm completely at the mercy of the forces of doom—"

"I am *not* your lucky charm! *Do you hear me, Justin?*"

He stopped and stared at her wildly. "But I love you, Agnes. I need you. I'm lost without you."

"Justin, you know that's not true."

"You don't understand!" He was nearly shouting, making alarmingly large, swooping gestures with the carving knife. "Without you I would have been killed. *What if it happens again?*"

"Try not to think about it. It won't happen again."

"How can you *know* that?"

"I just . . . I have a definite feeling."

"*A feeling isn't good enough!*" He was shouting now, despite knowing it didn't help. He took a deep breath, placed a jagged plank of pork on her plate, and began to spoon sauce over it with a shaking hand.

"I know you think I'm crazy but you must realize I can see certain things more clearly than you can. Terrible things are happening every minute of every day. They lie in wait and if you try to avoid them in one direction they spring up in another. Unless you're lucky. And that's the problem. *I'm not lucky*. At least on my own I'm not. With you it's different. You love me, you said so. And you saved my life, I don't know how you did it, but you did. And also you're so—" He faltered.

Agnes felt infinitely tired. She reached out and took his hand, wishing she were somewhere else.

"Justin, please try to listen. I don't want to be your lucky charm. I don't want to be some sort of metaphysical bodyguard. If I saved you once, it was coincidence, a once-in-a-lifetime thing. But I can't do it like a party trick, and I don't *want* to have to protect you at all, really. My life is complicated enough, though of course I'm happy to do what I can because you're my friend and I care about you, but it's been so difficult knowing how to help you lately. I *do* love you, in a way, because you're interesting and sweet—"

Justin winced.

"—but at the same time I'm quite worried about your mental state, and to be honest it probably was a bad idea that we had sex that time, even though it was very nice, because I'm not *in love* with you, and I'm sorry if that makes you feel bad because I know you've been through so much lately, but I have to say it because it's the truth." She peered at him and smiled a hesitant smile. "Don't look so sad, Justin, it's not the end of the world."

"Not yet." He looked away.

There was an uncomfortable silence. Justin broke it. "So, I want to be perfectly clear on this question. You're saying you're not in love with me?"

"Yes, that's exactly what I'm saying."

"You just thought it would be nice to take a few pictures to help make you famous and then dump me?"

Her eyes narrowed. "You know that's not true."

"Do I?" His voice took on a pleading tone. "Couldn't you try to be in love with me, just a little? I wouldn't be nearly so crazy if I knew you were in love with me."

"You can turn it on and off?"

"That's not what I meant."

"I know it's not. But look at yourself, Justin, you're bouncing around like a Ping-Pong ball. I can't save you, there aren't enough hours in the day. You'll get through it, I'm sure you will. You just need lots of time. Peace and quiet. Nothing to confuse you." She frowned. "Maybe you should see a doctor."

"No."

"A counselor?"

"*No.*"

"Would you consider going back home?"

He turned away.

"Well then . . . isn't there somewhere else?"

"You don't want me anymore." His voice was flat.

Agnes sighed. She had once liked the thought of helping him. She just hadn't realized how much help a person could require.

They ate dinner in silence. The pork was excellent.

"What about Peter and Dorothea?" she asked, putting the kettle on.

"What about them?"

She hesitated. "Maybe you could stay with them."

Justin nodded, defeated.

34

THERE WERE NO LAST WORDS when Agnes dropped him off at Peter's house.

She rang the bell, greeted Peter, said goodbye to Justin without touching him or meeting his eyes, and left. Justin was relieved that only Peter was present to witness his ignoble rejection.

Peter offered a quick tour of the house, explaining that his mother was usually first out in the morning, followed by the girls, that Justin would meet them all later, and in the meantime he should help himself to whatever he could find in the kitchen. Then he took his friend's bags up to the bedroom they would share, and left for school.

In contrast to the rest of the house, which was filled with

books and paintings and too many pieces of hopelessly mismatched furniture, Peter's room was spotless and noticeably devoid of stuff. It contained two single beds, a large bookcase stuffed nearly but not quite to overflowing, a map of the Milky Way that took up an entire wall, a colorful chart of the periodic table of elements, an impressive-looking refractor telescope, and a large note on the door that read FEED ALICE.

Justin wondered who Alice was.

He slowly unpacked his things, then wandered cautiously down to the kitchen, fixed himself four pieces of toast and Marmite, ate them slowly, and returned to Peter's room. He lay down and tried to read some of Peter's books, most of which dealt with the finer points of cosmology. He examined the telescope and wondered if it could be used to scan the neighborhood for suspicious characters. Then he gave up and fell asleep.

It was late afternoon when the sound of a cough woke him, and he struggled into a sitting position.

Peter's youngest sister (he guessed she was about six) stood in the doorway. She had bright blue eyes and fat pink cheeks, but the resemblance to Peter was indisputable. She gripped the end of a long slim plastic lead.

"Hello," she said, "I'm Anna. Peter says you're going to live here for a while."

Justin nodded.

She considered this for a moment. "Don't you have a family of your own?"

Justin sighed. "I do," he said. "But we don't really get on." He thought of Charlie with a pang.

"I don't always get on with my sister." She indicated

Dorothea, who had entered the room behind her, and dropped her voice to a whisper. "We can be quite horrible to each other."

Dorothea ignored her. "Hello again."

"Hello." He looked at the two girls. "I have a brother," he said.

"What sort of brother?" Dorothea looked interested.

"Quite a small one."

"Well," said Dorothea. "Small can be very exasperating. Do you miss him?"

Justin did, suddenly. "He's not a usual sort of child. He's quite unusual, in fact."

"In what way?"

He thought for a moment. "He seems to *know* things."

"Precocious." Dorothea shot a glance at Anna. "Very wearing."

Justin looked at the floor. "I also had a girlfriend."

"Had?"

"She hates me now."

Both girls gazed at him with interest. Then Dorothea seemed to remember something. "Peter said to ask about your dog."

"He's still missing. But he's not real anyway."

She considered this information. "What sort of not-real dog is he?"

"Greyhound."

"Hmmm. Might have been tricky. Might have been problems with the cats."

"And Alice," said Anna, brow furrowed with anxiety.

Justin said nothing.

"Well, we're glad you've come. Mum works much too hard so we're rather like orphans and could use the company. Will you cook for us?"

Justin nodded.

"Excellent. You're welcome to stay, then, as long as you're kind to Alice."

He considered the condition carefully. Perhaps it was a trick. Perhaps Alice was impossible to be kind to. "All right," he said finally.

Their faces relaxed into expressions of relief, as if the subject had been worrying them.

Dorothea extended her hand to seal the relationship.

He shook it.

"Your burn is better," she said, checking the palm of his hand, then turned to her sister. "Alice can come in now."

Anna tugged gently on the lead and a soft, sleepy-looking rabbit the size of a small mountain lion hopped slowly into the room.

"This is Alice," Dorothea said. "He'll be your pet." She looked at Justin dispassionately. "You need a rabbit just now. Alice, this is Justin."

Justin knelt on the floor and made a little clucking noise. The rabbit looked at him blandly.

"Stroke him like this," Dorothea said. She ran her hand firmly from the base of his ears to the middle of his back. "Otherwise he gets testy." Alice stretched to his full length and rolled over on one side with a little sigh of pleasure. Dorothea looked at Justin. "He's fairly safe as pets go, but be careful anyway. Things can happen with rabbits."

Justin stared at her. Things? What things? Singing-in-butcher-shop-type things? He shook his head to erase the image. "Why is he called Alice if he's a boy?"

"He just is." Dorothea looked at her watch, a fat digital with large numbers. "We have to go now, it's time to feed the cats. You'll find rabbit food in the shed behind the kitchen. Goodbye for now, Justin," she said with grave formality. "Good luck with Alice."

They left him alone with his pet.

Justin and Alice stared at each other. The rabbit twitched his ears. Justin looked deep into the large placid eyes, wondering what Alice was thinking. Alice gazed back at Justin, his expression mild.

Neither of them blinked.

Peter found them like that when he arrived home from school an hour later.

35

THE FIRST NIGHT they were awkward with each other. Despite a warm welcome from Peter's mother, Justin felt like a broken armchair that had been passed from house to house and was destined, eventually, for the dump. He didn't feel much like talking.

"I hope you're OK about living here," Peter said after he'd turned the lights out. "I mean, I know it's not your first choice."

Justin stared at the ceiling above his bed and said nothing for a while. "Why do you have a male rabbit called Alice?"

"Dorothea named him. I don't think she considered gender."

Justin sighed. "I had a bad experience with a rabbit once."

"Really?"

But Justin didn't elaborate, and for a while both boys lay awake thinking. Peter thought about the shape and behavior of the universe. Justin thought how he'd blown it with Agnes. How the only person on the planet who stood between him and further catastrophe had rejected him outright. How he was a goon and an oaf, and prone to hallucinations as well. How he was lousy at sex. She was probably with some older, more sophisticated friends at that very moment, laughing at his pitiable technique. He thought how pathetic it was to want to have sex with someone who despised you. He also thought about his brother. He missed Charlie, wondered if the child missed him too.

Eventually he fell into fitful unconsciousness.

The next morning, Justin remained in bed while the house rattled with action. He could hear Peter's mother and the girls, disorganized and noisy, and then Peter, quieter, on his own. Justin heard him moving about in the kitchen, and then he too was gone.

The silence of the empty house felt safe, reassuring; there were no complicated relationships to negotiate, no sexual snares, no emotional booby traps. He had been transplanted into a family, yes, but it wasn't *his* family.

For company, there was Alice. Within ten minutes of everyone's departure, Justin heard the thud thud thud of his heavy hops on the stairs, and then in the hall. When Justin opened the bedroom door, the rabbit looked up at him expectantly.

"Hello, Alice." Justin stood aside to let him enter and Alice hopped past him into the room, limbo-dancing his way under Justin's bed. Alice didn't take the place of Boy, but Justin liked his enormous, lumbering presence.

Justin stayed in bed, getting up only once to call his parents. They wanted phone numbers, addresses, and assurances that he was all right, but in the end they accepted his plan to stay with Peter a little longer, agreeing to inform the school that he would make up any work over the holidays. A few seconds before they hung up, Justin heard a click on the line, and there was something about the quality of the silence that made him hesitate.

"Charlie?"

The little boy's breathing was heavy with excitement.

"Hello, Charlie." Justin's pleasure gave way suddenly to guilt. How could he explain to his brother why he no longer lived at home? "I can't live with you just now, Charlie, but it's not because of you, it's because of all the disastrous things that might happen to me"? Or perhaps, "Don't take it personally, Charlie, it's just that I feel I'm going mad half the time and the rest of the time I feel nothing at all"?

"I'm sorry, Charlie." He felt his eyes well up. "I miss you."

It's all right, said Charlie. I miss you too. Come home when you can.

Justin could hear the little boy's breath, amplified by the mouthpiece he was holding too close. He smiled. "OK, then. Bye-bye."

"Bye-bye."

Neither of them moved.

"You can hang up the phone now, Charlie."

Justin waited for the click, replaced the phone carefully, and went back to bed. He couldn't think about his brother, not now. It made him want to cry. Instead, he buried his head in his pillow and slept through to the next day.

For a while the girls were cautious, respecting his privacy, whispering in barely audible voices outside his door and then creeping away disappointed. But as the days passed and he became more of a fixture in their lives, they became inquisitive and imperious, like robins.

Now they burst in, noisy and exuberant, with cold air caught between their layers of clothing, bearing exaggerated tales of the outside world. They cracked the door open if he didn't answer, and slid in, hiding under Peter's bed or in his wardrobe and talking in stage whispers until Alice and Justin emerged from their shared lassitude, lured out by the keen scent of a foreign existence. Alice maintained his appearance of dignified calm, but Justin's face lost a bit of its pallor at their approach.

Dorothea gave Justin inkblots and photographs to analyze. She listened intently to his answers, took careful notes.

"What do you see in this one?" she asked, showing him a black-and-white head shot of a pleasant-looking man in an old-fashioned fedora.

"It's the photograph on his obituary," Justin said. "He died in a terrible car crash and that's the picture his wife sent to the papers."

"What a strange answer," she said, frowning, her brow furrowed with concern. "You are a very unnatural person, Justin Case."

"You're not supposed to say it's strange," he answered. "You're supposed to say 'I see' in a nice calm voice and write it down."

"Yes, I *do* see. But it's still strange."

He nodded.

"What about this one?" She held up a picture of a prancing circus horse, festooned in brightly colored banners.

"No rider. He's fallen off. They can't stop the horse from galloping. It's running away. Gone mad. Rider brain-damaged. Or dead."

"You're making this up, aren't you?"

"I'm not. That's what I see."

"And this?" She held up an inkblot.

"I can't tell you. It's too gruesome." He turned away, shuddering.

Dorothea shook her head and made notes. "You make me look like Happy the Clown."

"I'm sorry."

She looked at him, surprised. "There's no need to be sorry. I don't imagine you *choose* to see the world this way."

They played word association, with predictably morbid results. At other times Dorothea followed Justin around with a notebook. She claimed to be studying (his) abnormal psychology.

"Do you suffer from bouts of melancholia?" Dorothea asked, then looked up at Justin and snorted. "Next question. Would you describe yourself as possessed by demons? Do you practice self-abuse? Have you thought of becoming a priest? What dreams do you have?"

Yes, yes, yes, no. His dreams were either too disturbing or

erotic to share so he made them up. "I dreamt I had a tiny dragon living in the palm of my hand. Its claws were extremely painful. It spoke with a squeaky voice and had razor-sharp teeth."

She scribbled "razor-sharp-teeth" into her notebook and underlined it twice, as Anna watched nervously, hugging Alice for safety.

"He *is* strange," Dorothea explained to Anna, "but not in a bad way."

If I could just stick by her, Justin thought. If I could just tell her all the things in my head, knowing my thoughts won't cause her to run away, or to wither. She doesn't think I'm mad, or at least she doesn't *show* that she thinks I'm mad.

It helped that at least a portion of someone else's reality overlapped his own.

And so, day by day, as Dorothea took notes and Anna clutched his arm, Justin fell in love with each of them a little more, with their soft bodies, blunt features, and strange fantasies; with their high voices and cat eyes and casual ways of demanding affection. It wasn't lust he felt, nor brotherly love, but something lighter and more ambiguous.

They, in turn, talked with him, followed him around, welcomed his presence in their lives.

They were little girls, but girls nonetheless.

36

JUSTIN MISSED HIS DOG.

As the days passed and Boy failed to reappear, Justin began to accept that he had been gravely wounded or killed in the airport explosion.

A disinterested observer might expect the death of an imaginary dog to be less traumatic than, say, the death of a real dog, but this was not the case. Justin felt that Boy was the only living creature who understood the peculiar half-reality occupied by his enemy. It made sense. Boy lived in that world too.

Yet if this was true, Justin brooded, if Boy had come to exist because he, Justin, had conjured him out of thin air, out of the murky depths of his subconscious, then how could Boy be killed off in the real world?

His head spun.

The dog had offered him solace and loyalty. Protection. Love. Boy was *his*, his creation, his companion. His soul mate. Boy was the only creature on earth who could fill the jagged void in his brain, in his heart. Who could possibly want to destroy that?

Justin knew. He dropped his head into his hands in despair.

I want my dog back.

I'll talk to him, he thought. I'll beg him to give me back my dog. I'll do anything. I'm not proud.

And then he sat up, suddenly angry.

But *I* created Boy. No one has the right to destroy him but *me*.

He was shouting now, spinning around like a blind boxer.

You can't just crawl into my head and destroy my creation! Do you hear me? He's my dog! He's mine, and I want him back!

Justin looked up and saw Dorothea staring at him. He brushed the tears from his face. Looked away.

"I was talking to fate."

She said nothing.

"I want my dog back," he explained.

"The greyhound?"

"Yes."

"Big pale gray dog?"

"Yes."

"Kind of brindly?"

"Yes."

"Wise eyes?"

"*Yes!*"

"I just saw him."

"What?"

"I just saw him in the back garden. He was staring at Alice. To be honest, I didn't entirely like the look in his eye. Greyhounds and rabbits, as I said before, not a great combination. But he didn't touch him. Just stared."

Justin bolted out of the room, down the stairs, and into the back garden.

No dog.

"DOROTHEA!"

"Yes?" She was standing beside him.

"Where did you see him?"

"Right there," she said calmly, pointing to a dense area of ferns by Alice's hutch.

And there he was, sprawled comfortably, half hidden by the foliage, head cushioned on a bag of wood shavings, asleep.

Justin grabbed Dorothea and hugged her.

"Thank you, Dorothea."

"For what?" she asked.

"For finding my dog."

She frowned at him. "I merely saw him. You brought him back."

37

WITH BOY'S REAPPEARANCE, Justin felt calmer, more connected to reality. That his reality encompassed an invisible dog and the occasional presence of the voice of doom seemed less significant than his ability to sleep at night, rise in the morning, and interact meaningfully with other human beings during the day.

This morning, from the kitchen window, he had seen a large muscular tabby prowling along the walls of the back garden. It disappeared suddenly, emerging from beneath a hedge with a mangled blackbird in its mouth. Though upset by the spectacle from the perspective of the bird, he admired the cat's ruthlessness, the way its lean belly hung from angular powerful shoulders and hips and nearly brushed the ground as it stalked.

"Have you seen Alice this morning?" Dorothea entered the kitchen, still in her nightdress, followed by Anna.

Justin nodded, stirring porridge on the front burner for Anna, and pointed to the outdoor hutch. "He's there, with Boy."

It was a mild morning and the greyhound lay in his favorite position, stretched out by the heating vent, watching over the hutch through one half-open eye while Alice hunkered somnolently, half buried in straw, secure in the presence of his bodyguard. Dorothea had been concerned that Boy would revert to the instincts of a natural cat killer, but since his reappearance he had seemed content just to observe; he barely acknowledged their presence.

"Well, that's a relief. It's been a terrible night," she said, her face grim. "You must have heard the cats. Nonstop yowling. The fox has the neighborhood all wound up."

Sightings of the fox that lived at the bottom of next door's abandoned garden occasioned great excitement and required special vigilance where Alice was concerned. Dorothea referred to the fox as a vixen, which puzzled Justin. How could she know? Surely a fox was a fox, especially at a distance.

"Don't be absurd," Dorothea chided him. "She's small, for one thing, and delicate around the chops. And for another, she's sneaky. She thinks like a woman."

Justin nearly laughed, but stopped in deference to Anna, who listened anxiously, her exaggerated terror mixed with a frisson of pleasure.

"What about *Alice*?" she gasped.

"Alice," Dorothea pronounced through clenched teeth and narrowed eyes, "is in danger. Because right now that fox smells *rabbit*."

Dorothea squinted out the window at the mangy red creature on the fence, then turned back to face Anna. "Once she has the scent of rabbit in her nostrils it's *curtains*." Dorothea grimaced horribly and drew her finger across her neck in a slicing motion.

Anna's face went blotchy with fear and her eyes filled with tears. "Poor Alice," she cried.

Dorothea shot her sister a look of contempt. "Don't be pathetic," she commanded disapprovingly. "It's Nature's way."

"*Alice!*" By now Anna was howling.

Dorothea threw Justin a look of infinite suffering, but Anna appeared so genuinely stricken that he felt obliged to step in.

"Don't worry, Anna. No fox in its right mind would take on a rabbit the size of Alice." He took her hot podgy hand in his two, and held it for a moment. Her answering gaze was full of devotion and the desire to believe him. When she looked at him that way he felt clear, almost luminous.

"Sentimental idiocy," Dorothea declared calmly. "Foxes eat rabbits. Doesn't matter how big they are. Predator and prey, that's the natural order of things. If the fox gets Alice, too bad. *That's his fate*."

Justin stared at Dorothea, who tilted her face away, triumphant.

All this fuss about one little life.
It's only a rabbit!

The fear switch in Justin's head flipped to ON.

Isn't it?

38

As THE DAYS PASSED, Justin propped himself between Boy and Peter, drawing strength from their constancy and discretion. He found that he could rest while Peter studied; his friend's even breathing and methodical page turning pacified him. Peter had the gift of moving quietly, of taking up so little space in a room that Justin often forgot the other boy existed, leaping startled to his feet when Peter made a noise. He began to see how successfully Peter's modesty deflected attention from whatever talents he possessed; the world seemed to flow around him silently, like water around a minnow.

Peter possessed, in fact, exactly the qualities Justin sought in vain to cultivate. Where Justin was anxious, Peter was calm.

Where Justin was murky, Peter was clear. Where Justin struggled to remove himself from fate's radar, Peter seemed to amble through life below it.

With the transparency bestowed on the pure of heart, Peter seemed unaware of himself, of his gifts. But Justin could think of little else. How was such clarity obtained? He would do anything to look like that, to have his face reflect the peaceful symmetry of an orderly soul. Sometimes he dreamt of a medical procedure, a specialized surgeon who would slit him from his thorax to his crotch, peel back the tarry layers of his epidermis, and insert a hose to suck out the gray areas, the filthy caves and murky darknesses that lurked around his heart, his stomach, his liver. What remained would be pink and healthy, springy and soft to the touch. It wouldn't stick to his fingers and stain his thoughts.

He'd lived with the Princes for a week when Peter suggested they train together. It seemed to Peter a good way to get his friend out of the house and reintroduce him to the world outside his own head.

Justin hesitated at first, but eventually gave in. So the two boys began to rise at a quarter to six each morning and set off in the winter gloom with Boy, at a steady pace of seven minutes per mile.

At first, Justin couldn't see the point. As much as he liked Peter, it was clear the boy was no athlete. He was far too tall and his sweats never seemed to fit properly; he spent the better part of every practice tugging at his waistband to keep it from slipping down around his knees. In addition, his gait was clumsy and lumbering, due partly to lack of coordination, Justin thought, partly to lack of vanity. Even in full flight, he lolloped sideways, perpetually off-balance and awkward.

And yet Peter never fell behind when they ran. At first Justin barely noticed. He'd adjusted his gait to match his friend's; it seemed impolite to live in a person's house and then leave him in the dust each morning. But after a few days Justin forgot to slow down, found himself working flat out. He arrived back at his new home streaming with sweat and puffing like a train. At his elbow, Peter wasn't even breathing hard.

When he ran sprints, Peter ran with him, often keeping up a cheerful line of patter that Justin had neither the breath nor the intellect to answer.

It took a long time for Justin to realize that he had never seen Peter tired.

Having made this observation, he upped the pace until their workouts left him staggering with exhaustion. He added miles to their morning run, then more miles, in an attempt to outrun the other boy. But still Peter loped along at his elbow without ever breaking into a sweat.

Finally, one Sunday morning, Justin stopped. He glared at Peter.

"What's this all about?"

Peter looked mystified. "Uh . . ." He shrugged. "I dunno."

"The running, Peter, the *running*. You never sweat."

Peter smiled apologetically and shrugged again. "I just don't really get tired."

"You don't get tired? What are you talking about? Of course you get tired. Everyone gets tired. Tired is what this is all about. I'm so tired right now I could throw up."

Peter nodded sympathetically. "Yeah."

"Yeah? What do you mean *'yeah'*?"

"I mean, I just don't get tired myself."

"*What?*" Justin shook his head. "Does Coach know this?"

Peter laughed nervously. "I . . . I don't think so. I never told him."

"What happens if you pick up the pace?"

"The pace? Um, not much."

"You *still* don't get tired?"

"Not really."

Justin gaped. "You're not fast, too, by any chance?"

"I don't know. I never timed myself."

"Come on, let's have a race, just a small one. Here to the end of the road." Above Peter's protests, Justin dropped to a crouch. "OK? Ready, go!"

Peter hesitated, starting well behind his friend, but in five strides had overtaken him. At a sprint, he turned to Justin. "Come on, this is ridiculous, let's not—"

Lungs bursting with the effort, Justin shouted, "RUN!"

Peter ran. He pulled away from Justin and began gaining ground, first one meter, then two. Boy bounded between the two boys joyfully—*now this is better!* Peter reached the end of the road first by nearly five meters, and Justin had seen him pull up at the end.

"Jesus, Prince," Justin choked, dropping exhausted to the curb. "Jesus." It took him a minute to be able to speak. "Coach'll drop dead when you tell him."

Peter looked uncomfortable. "I, uh, I'd rather he didn't know."

"What?"

"I'd rather you didn't tell him. He'll make me work harder and start shouting, or set me up as an example. I'd rather just do what I've always done."

Justin caught his breath. "I don't get it. If I could run like that I'd take out a full-page ad in the *Times*."

Peter Prince smiled. "No you wouldn't. And anyway, you're more coordinated. You look right. No one would be surprised if it were you."

They set off again—Peter, Justin, and Boy—more slowly now. Justin felt gloomy. What was the point of working so hard, running himself into the ground, when on either side of him was talent of a completely different magnitude?

"Don't you ever feel like running as fast as you can and winning, just to know how it feels?" he asked Peter as they puffed along in the flat morning light, the burn in his muscles reminding him of defeat.

Peter thought for a minute. "Not really. I guess if I wanted to win, I'd have done it before now. I hate the thought of being conspicuous."

"What does conspicuous have to do with anything? What about just running? What about running as fast as you can, just *for you*. Not for the applause or the medals or anyone else."

Peter didn't answer for a time. When he did, he was reluctant, shy. "I know what I can do."

"But why have a talent you don't use?" Justin knew he sounded petulant but couldn't help it.

"I do use it."

"You know what I mean. Why join the team?"

"I like the discipline, the routine." Peter paused. "I run because it feels graceful. It's the only time I don't feel like an auk. And it helps me think." He grinned at Justin. "Increases the blood supply to the brain."

They ran on in silence, crossing a road that on a weekday would be jammed with commuters. Now it was quiet except for a mail truck, a minicab driver in a shabby Ford, and a twenty-four-hour Laundrette attendant standing outside her shop smoking a cigarette. She waved as they passed.

"What about you?"

Justin sighed. "It wasn't my idea, I was sort of drafted. But it works. I do it . . ." He thought for a moment. "To escape, I guess. And also to keep me safe."

They ran in silence through a major intersection. Stopping for a red light, Peter looked sideways at Justin. "From fate?"

Justin nodded, defiant. "I don't care that everyone thinks I'm mad. I've had too many near misses."

Peter said nothing. Their feet hit the pavement in a careful, synchronized rhythm.

Justin looked straight ahead as he continued, his voice calmer, more resigned. "Only now I've changed into this other person who seems to be eating me alive. And most of the time I don't know which of us fate wants to kill."

Peter was silent for ten paces. Twenty.

"How do you know he wants you dead?"

Justin shook his head. "How do you know things? You just do."

"Bad science is always based on a convincing chain of logic," Peter mused. "Faulty logic, that is. Once it's in place, it's harder to unravel than no science at all. In order to disprove it, you have to take apart all the old evidence and try to figure out where the logic has gone wrong. With just one small deviation you get the sun revolving around the earth. Or influenza from breathing the night air."

"So?"

"So try rethinking your proposition. Check your logic. Are you running because you're being chased? Is something chasing you in order to do you harm? Think of a dog. What if fate is chasing you *because* you're running?"

"You believe me that he's real?"

"Not necessarily, but for this argument it doesn't matter. It's a bit like Boy. Even if the problem's all in your head, it doesn't change the dynamics of it."

"You think I should stop running?"

Peter looked thoughtful. "I don't know. I think you could stop being afraid. If there really is some supernatural force out to get you, you're not exactly going to fool it by pretending to be someone else. Or at least not for long. Why not go for an instinctive leap? Does it feel like it's working?"

"No."

Peter didn't say anything more, and for the rest of the run, there was no sound but breathing and the slap slap slap of feet on the pavement.

39

JUSTIN WENT BACK to school.

Rumors as to the reason for his absence had spread and despite—or perhaps because of—their vagueness, attracted new interest. One or two classmates swore they'd seen him in a photograph of the Luton air crash, but the newspaper pictures were small and badly printed, and it was impossible to be sure. A few teachers eyed him nervously, and he wondered what excuse his parents had come up with. Mental incompetence would at least have the benefit of being accurate.

He gave up any pretense of listening in class. Arriving when everyone else did, he composed his features into an expressionless blank, and while his teachers droned on about the Boer War and gravitational force, he thought about Agnes.

Occasionally he was singled out.

"Hey, goat boy."

"Mental Case."

But the majority of his peers couldn't be bothered.

Peter and Boy accompanied him nearly everywhere within school boundaries, and he was glad of the company. Peter had a kind of diplomatic immunity from harassment based on his intellect and his good nature, and Justin hoped some of it would rub off.

It was Peter who noticed that it was mainly the boys who saw Justin as a victim. The girls had gone uncharacteristically quiet.

Instead, they stared at him.

They stared at the black hollows around his eyes. They stared at his clothes, his indifferent way of wearing them, his haunted expression. They drifted towards him, towards his plane crash glamor and air of tragic sexuality.

And so he developed a following. Girls hovered near him from the moment he arrived at school each morning until the moment he left.

Justin noticed them milling about in his general vicinity. He eyed them suspiciously, expecting abuse. Instead, their eyes slid over him, paused, then flicked back again, alarmed and attracted by how much he wasn't like anyone else they knew.

They preened for him, rolled their hips, aimed newly grown breasts in his direction. They smoldered at him from flat, expressionless eyes.

He enjoyed the attention almost as much as he feared it.

“Hey,” said a leggy, world-weary fifteen-year-old.

Having no idea how to respond, he ignored her.

They interpreted his silence as mystery, imagined him tortured, passionate.

The fact of their interest aroused him. He had erections so often and so randomly that sexual desire became something to be endured, outlasted. He longed to give in to these girls, to the powerful certainty of their indifference. He longed to surrender to the intimacy of their cool, cruel hands.

And yet everything he knew about sex suggested it would only invite more humiliation. Another trap. It didn’t take much to imagine himself ensnared by lust. He was three-quarters there already.

Walking from one class to another, he looked up and saw Shireen and Alex, arms linked, parading through the halls with the absolute authority of Prime Minister and Lord High Chancellor.

We run this principality, their hip-rolling sexually satisfied strut said.

As they passed him, Shireen stopped. Then she turned slowly, as to the lowliest serf in the filthiest hovel in the darkest of the Dark Ages, and with a single flash of her perfect almond-shaped eyes and a flare of her exquisite nostrils, she annihilated him, turned her phasers on the space he occupied and Zap! made it empty.

He drifted, vaporized, to the library, found the bleakest most uninhabited corner, and settled. A few random molecules with a wounded soul. He didn’t take up much room.

All around, people of average density came and went—walking near him, through him, hiding for a quick snog, swapping cigarettes or joints, sending illicit texts. One actually glanced at a book.

He noticed that a girl had followed him, was watching him.

Another fan, he thought bitterly, and drifted away through a wall of books before he had a chance to see that she had ventured, ever so slightly, to smile at him. It was a good smile, without subtext.

Sliding down into a tiny heap by a pile of daily newspapers, he closed his dematerialized eyes and tried to console himself with his relatively privileged position in the world order. He knew from the headlines beside him that people were starving in countries with few natural resources. That earthquakes and freak storms killed thousands, while despots and fanatics turned their people into slaves, murdered children, tortured doctors.

Peter was right. Compared to them, he was the luckiest person on earth. Unloved and unlovable perhaps, but comfortable, well fed, in command of his faculties. Not blind, not lame, not culturally handicapped in any way. Unless you counted the rubber circus ball on which he constantly scrambled for balance; the perpetually shifting, rolling ground beneath him.

He gathered himself up and left the library.

If only he could run away, cruise through the boundaries where neighborhoods became outskirts and outskirts became farms; where pavements became verges became hedgerows and the ground beneath him turned soft and springy with leaf mold. He needed proof of the density of his bones and the elasticity of his muscle. He needed a regular driving pace to strengthen his spirit, to set up an orderly percussion in his brain.

He ran alone, faster, harder, longer; racing his libido to kingdom come and back again. He ran to wring the lust from his limbs, exhaust his brain of terror and desire. He ran to stop thinking of silky hair and silky thighs, of bleeding stumps and icy lips, of screams and moans and whispered threats. He ran so that exhaustion would permit him to sleep. He ran to escape the inexorably, terrifyingly natural path of his fate.

It didn't work, of course, but at least he was too tired to stay awake all night whacking off.

40

AGNES DIDN'T PHONE at all during Justin's stay with Peter and Dorothea. She felt it was kinder that way, though in fact it wasn't. When she finally did make contact, she was greatly relieved that it was Peter who answered the phone.

"I'm having a show." She sounded excited. "I've had an idea for some time now." After a few minutes of general chat, she rang off, without asking to speak to Justin.

Peter felt a knot of worry form in his stomach, but there was nothing he could say, nothing to do but wait and see. When he passed the message on to Justin over breakfast the next day, he played down the news, but Justin's nonchalance fooled no one.

"What exactly made you fall in love with Agnes?" Dorothea asked him, accepting a piece of toast.

Peter glanced at his friend.

"She made me feel important. Like I was fascinating. And she's so"—he paused—"so absolute. I was flattered."

"Hmmm."

"What do you mean, 'hmmm'?"

"Just hmmm." Dorothea chewed thoughtfully for a minute. "And that's enough to make a person fall in love?"

"Being flattered? I guess it was for me. She spent a lot of time looking deep into my eyes and coming up with ways to improve me. I guess that sounds pathetic."

"Yes." Dorothea's gaze was impassive.

Justin paused, the bread knife clutched in one hand. "Maybe it depends how desperate you are to be improved."

"How desperate are you?"

"Oh, way off the scale," he said. "More toast?"

Peter placed a bowl of cat food out by the back door. "You might be average for all you know. Other people conceal it better."

"Concealing it better *is* less desperate."

Dorothea shook her head. "Being you must be horrible."

"Thanks a lot." Justin looked depressed.

"Never mind. Not much you can do about it anyway." Brushing the crumbs off her nightdress, she swapped her slippers for wellies, and strode off down the garden to the bird table with a fistful of bread crusts.

The next time Agnes phoned, it was to tell Justin and Peter

she needed to get away for the day, and did they want to come with her to the seaside? Open vistas, stormy seas, and gray skies were what she required. Empty space. The sea.

"I thought it would be nice to have you both," Agnes said.

You've already had me, Justin thought mirthlessly. You want to have him, too?

"Justin?"

But it's December, he thought. It'll be freezing cold and bleak and lonely, which is probably why you don't want to go by yourself. And anyway, haven't you got any playmates your own age?

"Yes, fine," he said. She didn't want to be alone with him, that much was clear. Peter, however, seemed pleased to have been included. So the following Saturday, under an early-morning sky lit with brilliant sunshine filtered through dark gray clouds, they set off to Agnes's flat.

Thanks to the proximity of the Christmas season, Luton was at its most garishly festive. They took a detour through the mall, shielding their eyes from the blast of silver glare as they entered. The PA system gushed music so distorted it was impossible to tell what song was playing. It might have been "Good King Wenceslas," though it also sounded a little like "Santa Baby."

Boy whimpered and pressed himself against Justin's leg.

Peter and Justin looked around, and then back at each other, eyes wide with mock horror.

"Run!" Peter shouted, and they did, bursting through the

automatic doors and collapsing with laughter outside. "Oh my god. It's like the ninth circle of hell in there."

"There's a present I need to find for Charlie," Justin said. "I've looked everywhere else, but I can't face that place."

Peter nodded. "Nightmare. All Christmas shopping is."

They walked together towards Agnes's house, squinting into the sun in a companionable silence. Peter occasionally tossed a soggy shredded toy ring for Boy. The dog didn't bother chasing it, just reached up with each throw and caught it a few inches from his head, returning it to Peter with an air of dutiful resignation.

When they were nearly there, Peter turned suddenly to his friend.

"Justin," he began tentatively, "I've been wondering exactly what happened between you and Agnes. I mean, if you don't mind my asking. You seemed to get along, and then . . . why was there such a rush to move in with us?"

At another time, the question would have plunged Justin into despair, but now he only sighed. "We had sex. I told her I loved her. It was a disaster."

Peter looked thoughtful. "Women are tricky," he said, taking the ring from Boy and throwing it again as they turned down Agnes's street. "Of course I'm only guessing here. My experience with women is fairly limited. Very limited, actually." He laughed. "In fact, it begins and ends with sisters."

"Mine begins and ends with humiliation."

"Wasn't it worth it?" Peter's interest was genuine.

"Not unless you're a sucker for rejection."

They rang the bell and Agnes shooed them through to the living room while she finished getting dressed. Peter and Justin found themselves sitting awkwardly together on Justin's old bed, a fact they both attempted to ignore.

"Hey, cheer up," Peter whispered once Agnes had left the room, "at least you've had sex."

"It's had me, more like."

Peter wondered why people so rarely appreciated the complexities of the moment. He wondered what it would be like to have lost his virginity, to be attractive to women, to possess whatever quality it was about Justin they found so hypnotic.

Peter thought he knew what it was. There was something about his friend's uneasy blackness that mesmerized him, too: Justin's neediness, his desire (and his inability) to make two plus two equal anything but pi. He appeared utterly incapable of ordering the universe in a reassuring manner; had trouble differentiating hunger from loneliness, anger from love, fear from desire. Peter couldn't imagine going through life with a brain so peculiarly wired, but it made compulsive viewing. Like watching a train crash.

Anger and fear reentered the room dressed in a bright green ankle-length oilskin coat, an absurdly long cable-knit Aran scarf, and white high-heeled rubber boots.

"What do you think?" Agnes asked. "No, don't tell me, I won't have anyone being rude about my country clothes."

Peter grinned at her. "The coat is very nice. I wish I had one like it."

Justin sulked.

"Where are we going, by the way?" he grumbled. "Are you

taking us to Beachy Head? Planning to lure us to the edge, push us over, then swear blind it was an accident?"

"Exactly," Agnes said. "Especially if you continue being such a spoilsport."

She held the door open for them and followed with the car keys, a picnic box, and a little furry bag full of maps. "Come along, boys, adventure beckons."

41

JUSTIN HAD NEVER DRIVEN with Agnes before. He sat crammed into the backseat of her ancient Renault with Boy, who had adopted his usual position of splendid languor: head comfortably in his master's lap, back pushed up against the nubbly old fabric of the car's backseat, legs outstretched.

Justin sat with his hands over his ears to block out the whine of the car as it strained to compete on the motorway. He was glad he couldn't see the road; Agnes drove neither wisely nor well.

Although Peter's height made his occupation of the front seat obvious, he had tried to insist that Justin sit next to Agnes. Justin would have accepted the offer if he could possibly have done so without appearing childish. Now he could see the two of them chatting easily, their words swallowed by the noise of the engine.

What was he doing here anyway? He couldn't remember what he'd ever seen in Agnes, that hard-hearted scheming harpy, seducer and abandoner of innocent youth. Boy glanced at him sideways and Justin glared back.

With Peter's enthusiastic support, he opened Agnes's picnic after an hour on the road, distributing crisps, sandwiches, and bananas despite her protests.

"How depressingly English to eat in the car," she sighed. "I brought blankets and hot coffee for the beach."

For an instant Justin imagined the freezing beach—the three of them huddled together, inhibitions taking second place to warmth—and regretted the spoilt picnic.

It shouldn't have taken much more than two hours to reach the coast, but the combination of Agnes's map reading and driving skills meant it took three. She and Peter were exuberant, but Justin continued to sulk. The longer he sulked, the more he felt like a fool, but he was unable to turn back with grace.

They left the A road. There was enough warmth in the early-winter sun to color the reedy landscape gold, and, pressing his face to the back window, Justin saw a handful of vivid copper-colored horses half hidden behind screens of hedgerow. One of them looked up and watched them pass, throwing its head high against the damp wind.

The scrub changed to salt marsh, with teasels and tall feathery grasses. A great blue heron flapped its prehistoric wings and rose heavily into the sky. Justin could smell the sea in the cold wind whistling through the window. There were terns, flitting and diving, and egrets wading in the marshy plain.

Agnes turned, finally, onto a dirt path marked PRIVATE and they bumped along parallel to the coast, past a large, stern Edwardian house surrounded by incongruously green lawns. The road ended in a circle of cleared sand signposted NO PARKING. Agnes stopped the car, got out, pulled on her bright green oilskin, and stretched her arms out into the wind.

"What a view!"

She pointed out past the scrubby dune and Justin saw the top third of a large red sail gliding mysteriously along behind it on what appeared to be sand. He held the car door open for Boy, who stepped carefully to the ground, stood poised for a moment, eyes half closed, then shot off like a rocket over the dune to the beach beyond.

The icy salt air and the warm sun made Justin feel exultant too. He nearly forgot his grudge in the desire to follow Boy down to the beach.

"Come on," he called to Peter, and they ran. Agnes brought up the rear, surprisingly agile in her high-heeled boots, and the three arrived at the crest of the hillock together. A narrow channel of deep water explained the sailboat, and curlews stood further out in the muddy shallows, poking their long beaks into the water in search of lunch. A hundred meters down the beach, Boy had skidded to a halt and appeared to be practicing airs above the ground, leaping and hovering, legs outstretched like a Lipizzaner. As Justin watched, his dog rolled in a pile of seaweed, shook himself free of his city smells, stood trembling for a moment in the sun, then shot off again across the dunes.

Justin flopped down in the tall pale grass, pulled his arms up into the warm sleeves of his coat, and closed his eyes while Peter wandered down to the water.

"As there's no picnic, I'm going to walk," Agnes said, pointing south along the coast to where the mudflats gave way to a shimmering pebble beach. "If by any chance I lose you, we'll meet back here before sundown."

Justin nodded without opening his eyes; the winter sun on his face made him lazy.

Click click click. He ignored her.

Peter came back up from the sea, his shoes and the bottoms of his trousers damp with salt water. He wanted to tell Justin how nice and friendly he found Agnes, but remembering his friend's mood, thought better of it. "Shall we walk?" he said instead, turning to follow the little path through the dunes.

Justin stood up slowly, dozy and languid, and tramped after him.

They followed the coast down to where the dunes met the sea. It was easier to stick to the path than to walk on stones, but it required them to balance sideways against the wind that flew straight at the coast, swept up the hills of sand, gusted across the marshes and ruffled the reed beds. Justin stuffed his hands in his pockets and pulled his knit cap down over his ears. He looked over at Peter—head thrown back, hatless, coat flapping in the wind—and shook his head.

"Aren't you freezing?"

"No. I'm warm-blooded. I like cold air rushing through my brain, remember? Makes it think harder to keep warm."

"You're mad."

Peter grinned, punch-drunk on sea air.

Justin followed the path down to a shelf of shale. The wind dipped, and he stopped at a rock pool, squatting to get a closer look. It was illuminated by slanting rods of sunlight and appeared still except for a slight ripple on the surface. He felt the water. It was warm.

Justin lay flat and lowered his face to within an inch of the surface, imagining himself floating through the weeds. He breathed out gently, ruffling the surface, then held his breath, waiting for the water to clear. Through half-closed eyes, he projected himself down, down into the pool, until he was gliding through unexpectedly warm winter eddies, safe in his tiny, enclosed world.

There were dark red sea anemones at the bottom, opening and closing slowly like mouths. They looked gentle and welcoming. He swam around and looked deep into one of them, stroking the velvet red flesh of its throat. At the base of a reed, a periwinkle glided, leaving a faint trail in the sand. Now he could see a small population of crabs tiptoeing back and forth with the soft rocking of the pool; now a handful of tiny minnows surrounded him, curious, bumping him with their weightless bodies.

A cloud covered the sun and Justin felt suddenly cold. He stood up and left the little ecosystem, following Peter's footprints along the beach. He could see his friend walking down along the water. Agnes was nowhere to be seen. Even the mile of curving bay showed no trace of her. Perhaps a shining pit of pebbles had swallowed her up.

Justin stopped to watch a group of cormorants fish from a half-submerged boulder in the sea, and when he resumed his walk, Peter, too, had disappeared. It seemed ages before he and Boy found him again, unexpectedly, huddled down in a sheltered dip between two dunes.

Boy flopped down in the sand, head diagonally across his front paws, and watched drowsily as Peter flipped the pages of a small well-worn book on coastal geology.

"Hi," said Peter, moving over to make a space for Justin. "I'm just reading about Baltic amber. Apparently this whole coast is littered with it. The book says people have been collecting it here for centuries but I've been looking all day and can't find any. It's a strange little text, listen to this," he said, searching for a page. "It says: 'Baltic amber, fifty million years old and full of fire; warm, and enduring like love.' Wonderfully romantic, don't you think? Only, I don't know how to differentiate the stuff from plain old yellow stones."

He poured a handful of yellow pebbles into Justin's palm. "Hold them up to the light. If it's amber, you can see through it."

Justin held one after another up to the light. They were nothing but stones. "I wish we'd saved some of that picnic. I'm starving."

"Me too. I'm going to keep looking for amber. We don't have to turn back just yet."

He pushed himself to his feet and set off again, leaving Justin and Boy huddled together in the dip. The sun sat low in the sky, but the little sheltered spot was perfectly situated to trap what was left of the weak rays. Justin lay back against the bank of warm sand, dreaming of amber. The temperature would begin to drop soon; Boy was already wedged up against him for body heat.

A few minutes later he saw Agnes and Peter returning, walking close together. Agnes stopped occasionally to examine a shell or snap a picture of Peter, and Justin felt a wave of jealousy.

So that's what this little outing was all about, he thought. Yet one more opportunity to remind me that anyone will do.

He flipped over, pressed his face downwards, and blinked, feeling his eyelashes brush across the sand. Turning slightly, he could see Peter and Agnes squatting at the water's edge, laughing. They didn't look in his direction, and after a minute they passed out of sight. He could have kept them in his line of vision, but rejected the impulse.

Boy shivered and looked at Justin inquiringly.

"OK," he sighed, reluctant to move from the safety of his secluded niche. "Let's head back."

He walked slowly, picking up every yellow stone he saw. Most remained stubbornly opaque in the sunlight; a few were translucent but heavy and cold. One by one he tossed them into the sea. He liked the hollow *bloop* they made as they broke the surface of the water.

It must be one of those tales, he thought, turning back to the beach, like mermaids singing.

As they neared the end of the beach, Justin drifted closer to the sea, where the pebbles glittered in the last low rays of the sun.

And then without any signal or obvious sign of transformation, the beach was suddenly alight with fiery stones. Where seconds ago he had seen nothing, they now glowed against the opaque pebbles like little beacons.

Hands trembling, Justin picked one up and held it to the light. The complex center revealed itself at once. He closed his fist around the ancient drop of sap, smoothed by the sea and set alight by the sun. It was light and warm in his hand.

In a burst of excitement, Justin picked up one after another until he held twelve glowing drops of flame in his hands. Each revealed a different internal landscape, from palest yellow to a reddish marbled gold.

And then the sun moved and they were gone.

He searched the shoreline, frantic, in vain. The sun had dropped below the horizon and the entire beach was thrown into shadow. Justin stood motionless, watching the glow fade from the sky, taking with it the last faint flickers of warmth.

Boy appeared at his side and he held the stones out to the greyhound, who sniffed at them delicately, then turned away, unimpressed.

Justin stood cradling his handful of warm stones. Then he headed back towards Agnes through the fading light.

42

ON THE WAY BACK they stopped for dinner at a pub with dark varnished beams and flashing fruit machines. They found an empty table and ordered sausage and mash from the bar. The gas fire in the little saloon bar managed to throw out enough heat to make them drowsy. None of them felt inclined to speak, so they ate in silence.

"Did you find your amber?" Justin asked Peter, through a mouthful of Agnes's treacle pudding.

Peter reached into his pocket. "I guess I'll have to come back. I found something that looks right, but I think it's yellow quartz."

Justin took the small yellowish stone from Peter. It looked

as if you might see through it, but it was heavy and cold. Lifeless.

He shrugged and gave it back.

They drove home in silence. Justin would have fallen asleep with Boy's head in his lap had it not been for the roaring of the motorway and the icy sliver of wind blowing down his neck through the loose window. Instead, he stared out into the blackness at the double pinpoints of light traveling in the opposite direction and thought about amber.

Warmth, he thought. And brilliance. Transparency.

Timing, too. Peter telling him what to look for.

Fifty-million-year-old sap.

Five minutes of illumination.

The sun at just the right height.

Chance. A series of events, combined to make a coincidence. Leading to a revelation.

He could have walked on that beach forever without noticing its treasures.

Perhaps his past and his future were also hidden somewhere on the beach, carved onto a single pebble, a Rosetta Stone with the key to the whole of his existence. Perhaps all the answers lay dormant somewhere, waiting to be discovered.

Justin thought of all the events of his life, collecting and dispersing like a handful of dust. Things happened and didn't happen a billion times a second.

How many events add up to a coincidence?

How many coincidences add up to a conspiracy?

"Justin?" Agnes called softly, searching for eye contact in

the rearview mirror. "We're nearly home. Peter's fast asleep. Why are you so scrunched up in the corner?"

He didn't talk to Agnes about Boy. And so he didn't answer, just frowned in the darkness. He stretched his cramped muscles as best he could without disturbing his dog.

"I'm so glad you came," she said, her voice intimate, despite the rattling car. "I knew you'd like it there."

He nodded again, but inside he felt cold.

Of course you knew I'd like it. You know so much about me, so much more than I do. You know what's real and what's not. What's useful and what's not. What endures and what's just for one night.

So many things you know about me.

Agnes stopped the car in front of Peter's house and he woke up immediately, the sudden absence of racket deafening. They all squeezed out of the car and stood, dazed and a little awkward, by the front gate.

"Good night," said Agnes, kissing Peter on the cheek. But Justin backed away, afraid of the smell of her hair and the feel of her skin. The two boys began walking stiffly up the path.

"Justin!" called Agnes after him, and he turned back. "Justin, please don't be angry with me." She caught up and took his arm, pulling him close. He didn't move away and they remained at an impasse a few seconds too long, unable to move forwards or back until finally Justin pulled free, dug a piece of amber out of his pocket, and placed it in her hand, closing her fingers around it.

"Here," he said. "Amber." Warm and enduring like love, he thought, his heart contracting.

Before she could say anything, he had disappeared into the house. Agnes sat in the front seat of her little car with the amber in her hand for some time before starting the engine again.

Justin and Peter undressed at opposite ends of the room and shut off the lights without speaking. It was still early, but the long walk and salt air had left them feeling windswept and tired.

Peter fell asleep immediately and dreamt of a beach littered with fiery stones.

Justin returned to the warmth and safety of his rock pool and floated there weightless in the winter sunlight until dawn.

43

ON THE EVENING Agnes's show was due to open, Ivan took the train up from London with a group of friends he'd hijacked to accompany him. He told them not to expect much: a small collection of photographs and fashion in Luton, ha ha. It was hardly going to set the world alight. But Agnes was his friend, after all. There was such a thing as loyalty.

The Londoners arrived at Luton Station like a flock of geese, squawking and huddling together in a noisy gaggle, pecking nervously at the disorientating suburban vision around them.

"Dear, dear," Ivan said, eyebrow raised. "So this is what Kansas looks like."

One of the stylists gripped his arm and wobbled slightly on her stiletto heels. "It's called the suburbs, darling."

"Isn't there some sort of government rescue initiative?"

"Of course not. They like it like this."

He snorted. "Impossible."

The woman shrugged. And then with a great deal of swearing that they would never again leave the safety of the big city, they piled into a small fleet of taxis and made their way to the gallery.

Agnes was there to greet them, wearing a short sky blue wool pinafore shot full of tiny holes. Each hole was beautifully backed with red felt and stitched and finished in black surgical silk. On her head she wore a little felt hat hung with tiny glass and metal charms. As she moved, she tinkled gently like a wind chime. A narrow unraveling scarf with a little glove at each end trailed down her back and onto the floor.

Ivan's crowd sniffed grudgingly at her outfit and began to peer around.

Agnes had chosen her best photographs of Justin and blown them up to eight-by-three-foot panels. There were four sets of three panels, twelve portraits of Justin in total. Six pictures ran down each side of the gallery, the gigantic figures looming over the empty white space. On the far wall were three extra panels forming a triptych, like an altarpiece. The three panels in the triptych were photographs taken during the airport crash: melting windows and tangled limbs, burning metal, tormented faces, severed body parts, and Justin, always Justin. Justin smiling weirdly at the scene of the disaster. Justin confused, Justin angry, Justin lost. The vertical format meant that each photograph encompassed floor, windows, and ceiling of the airport terminal. They gave Agnes's compositions a sense of spatial grandeur that brought to mind early-Renaissance paintings.

Around the room, soft, featureless mannequins wore Agnes's clothing designs. They were fashioned like huge headless rag dolls out of white muslin and wore felt gloves in innocent bright colors, each with a ragged edge where it looked as if fingers had been severed. There were linen shirts with the arms torn off, pale pink leather bags lined in red silk that Agnes had pulled in long fraying streams through small slits in the surface of the skins. Sweaters and T-shirts were perforated, the holes stitched carefully along the edges with surgical silk and backed with red fabric.

It was beautiful. And deeply unsettling.

Justin arrived by way of the mall, where he had stopped to shop for his brother. He'd been on the verge of giving up the search, but today had girded his loins, braved the mall, and found exactly what he wanted. When he asked them to wrap it, he was directed to the queue at the Christmas wrap table, where he waited half an hour with a dozen other disgruntled shoppers.

When finally he reached the front of the queue, the official wrapper took one look at his gift and demanded double payment. "It's not regulation size," she said with distaste, "and it's the wrong shape. And it won't go in a bag, either."

Next year, thought Justin, handing over his four pounds, I'll get the kid a pile of bricks if it'll make your job easier.

It was only after he left the mall that Justin realized he was stuck with the package for the evening. At more than a meter long, covered in reindeer paper and tied with a huge green and silver bow, it would not contribute to the air of casual insouciance he had hoped to convey.

He met Peter and Dorothea outside the gallery. Peter had placed himself carefully in front of the show's title on the front window, and a smiling Agnes pushed through the crowd to greet them. She kissed Peter, but Justin took a step backwards and Dorothea managed to make herself look unkissable. The atmosphere in the little group was tense; none of them quite dared look beyond Agnes to the walls, which left them nowhere to put their eyes.

Agnes glanced at Justin's parcel.

"Don't worry," he sighed wearily, "it's for my brother." *Not some kind of pathetic attempt to win you back.* "I don't suppose there's anywhere to put it down." Justin's eyes skated off in search of a coatroom, accidentally encountering twelve large panels mounted with gigantic representations of himself on the way.

He brought his eyes back very slowly to meet hers, emptying them of expression in the process. And then, even more slowly, he took in what she was wearing: the unraveling scarf around her neck with the tiny hands knit into each end, the little red holes, the delicate shards of metal and glass tinkling on the dome of her hat. He took in the entire vision of Agnes dressed in postmodern disaster-victim chic surrounded by portraits of her moody, miserable spurned lover, her discarded, distressed virgin youth, who happened also to be present here, in the flesh, conveniently clutching (for maximum dramatic—or perhaps comic—effect) an oversized, garishly wrapped soft toy.

Him, in other words.

Agnes had chosen her portraits precisely, presented him sad, confused, and blank. She had displayed him at his most vulnerable and beseeching. He looked incontrovertibly pathetic.

Doomed Youth, indeed. When he had contemplated his doom, it had never occurred to him it would be like this, would play out here, in a brightly lit room surrounded by people.

"What do you think?" Agnes chirped, much too brightly.

Justin stood very still. He said nothing. Boy gazed up searchingly at Agnes's face. Dorothea didn't breathe, and Peter had to turn away from the spectacle of pain seeping out and pooling at his friend's feet.

"Look, Justin . . ." she began, but just then heard her name called, and retreated with evident relief.

"Do you want to leave?" Dorothea whispered.

Justin still said nothing.

"Come on," Peter said, with an Englishman's courage under fire. "Now we're here, we may as well look around."

As the little group moved into the gallery, Justin caught sight of a dress sewn all over with tiny red dots. Blood, he thought, horrified. *It's spattered with blood.* He shuddered and turned away, to a linen shirt with a jagged tear where one of the arms should be.

Justin froze, his face a mask. A buzz spread through the room; once someone had made the connection between the boy in the coat and the photographs of the boy in the coat, his presence attracted the attention of the entire company. "He's good-looking," someone whispered, "but obviously *not quite himself*."

On the contrary, Agnes thought, he is *quite himself*.

Peter came up beside her. "You should have told him."

She folded her arms, defensive. "How could I?"

Peter said nothing.

"I do love him, you know." She paused and looked around the room. "Just not in the way he wants me to." Her voice had a petulant note.

So that's how it is, Peter thought. Justin, desperate to be loved, and Agnes, desperate to be absolved of blame.

Despite their cruelty, the photographs of Justin were beautiful. Agnes had captured the hesitant nerviness that lurked just beneath his friend's fine translucent skin. The pictures pierced Justin like X-rays, peeled back the flesh to expose a soul so raw it could have revealed itself only in trust and love.

The way he looked at the camera was the way he looked at Agnes.

Peter moved away, embarrassed, as if he'd witnessed something private.

The plane crash scenes came almost as a relief with their depictions of clear, unambiguous horror. It was a more comfortable sort of voyeurism. How terrible, one could think. How wrong, how painful, how tragic. And how expressive, how courageously witnessed. He had to admit that Agnes had presented something piercingly true in the juxtaposition of tragedy and victim.

Peter had turned back to the crowded room, scanning it for familiar faces, when he saw Justin pushing his way through the gallery towards him.

The triptych was crowded with spectators, but even before Justin could see the entire work, his brain filled in the missing pieces of the panels from memory. Slipping quietly, insistently, to the front, overcome with something between outrage and fear, he already knew what he would find there.

These pictures. She should never have . . .

Have what? Taken them? Printed them? Shown them?

Yes.

He scanned the room for Agnes, and, shoving his way through to her, wrapped his hand tightly around her upper arm and dragged her away from a small group of acolytes.

"What were you thinking, Agnes? It's horrible." He glared at her, eyes burning. "*You're* horrible. What have you done? You've turned me into some kind of freakish spectacle. *And you didn't even ask me*." He felt as if he'd been turned inside out, stripped of all dignity, and exposed to a leering public. The fury overtook him in waves; he wanted to kill her, himself, everyone in the room.

"I'm sorry, Justin. I should have warned you." She sounded defensive. "But I *made* something of it. That's all."

"You *made* something? Of *corpses*? Of *me*?"

She followed his eyes over her shoulder to a suit jacket that had been sliced to pieces, then stitched roughly back together with brown string.

Justin collected himself. "I have to go now, I just wanted to stop for a minute."

Someone interrupted Agnes and she turned away, leaving Justin tumbling slowly towards the exit. There appeared to be plenty of time as he fell, time to experience quite distinct waves of anger and disgust.

"Justin . . ." Agnes called after him without much conviction. She didn't add "wait."

He opened the door, and the gallery coughed him out into the street.

44

OUTSIDE, bathed in the faint greenish light of a winter thunderstorm, Justin ducked his head against the frigid wind. From the shadows, puffing calmly on a cigarette, Ivan watched, amused.

So, Agnes hadn't told him he was the star of her little show? Tch, tch. Shocking omission. Well, there's no such thing as a free shag, Justin, my boy. There's a lesson for you, for next time.

Justin raised his head to look back through the heavy plate glass. Everywhere he looked, his own image stared back, twice as large as life, mocking him.

It's not me, he felt like shouting. That person isn't *me*. The need to rid himself of the person in the photographs, to destroy the hideous, pitiable figure in the beautiful gray coat, took him over until there was nothing left but rage. And so as it began to rain, big icy drops that made the grimy road dangerously slick, he peeled off the precious garment and hurled it as hard as he could. It landed flat and heavy under a steady stream of sleet and traffic.

"Let's get out of here," he said to Boy, and began to run, head ducked, his brother's Christmas present pressed to his chest, shirt collar pulled up against the rain. If he'd waited another few seconds, he might have seen Ivan dive into the road after his coat with a furious oath. He might have heard the skid and screech of tires and seen the stormy oblivious world close over the man one last time, seen the sodden coat and its maker become indistinguishable from roadkill.

But Justin's head was down and it was dark. It was all he could do to keep upright against the driving needles of freezing rain. Which is how he came to collide with a middle-aged woman walking towards him on the pavement. Her head and neck were stiff and painful and she walked quickly, eyes downcast, anxious to be home in bed. The rain stung her face and ran down into her eyes, a tiny percentage pooling and mixing with fluids contained in the conjunctiva.

In the exact moment of the glancing impact of Justin's body against her own, she blinked, and momentum caused a drop of fluid from the mucous membrane surrounding her eye to traverse the few inches into Justin's slightly open mouth. It was the sort of event that happens a thousand times a day—on trains, in lifts, wherever strangers in close proximity cough, or sneeze or shake hands.

In its entirety, the encounter lasted about two seconds.

Justin, soaked and freezing, regained his balance, mumbled an apology, and continued to run. At Peter's house, he toweled off his dog, threw a blanket on the floor, placed his brother's gift on the radiator to dry, stripped off his own clothes, ran a hot bath, and lay in it until his bones thawed, his fingertips accordioned into whitish folds, and the water began to cool. Then he dried himself and crawled into bed beneath a pile of quilts, his steaming body warming the cold sheets.

Peter, Dorothea, and Anna arrived home soon afterwards, and Justin could hear them at the doorway to the bedroom, whispering. They waited for a sign that he wanted company but he gave none, and eventually the whispering ceased.

The next time Justin awoke he could hear Peter's calm, regular breathing across the room, and the dial of his watch glowed 2 a.m. He lay awake then, disturbed by images of disembodied limbs and torsos riddled with shrapnel, legs with no feet, fingerless hands.

The memory of Agnes's photographs sickened him.

He came down that morning thickheaded and depressed, and found Dorothea and Anna already awake, feeding the cats and talking about Agnes. He asked Dorothea, cautiously, what she thought of the show.

"It's very clever in some ways," she answered coolly. "And the photographs of you are beautiful, even when you look your worst. Most people won't care that it's all very horrible as well. They'll just think it's new and different and terribly original." Dorothea's eyes were unsentimental. "I'm not wild about her angle on friendship, if that's your question. She's treated you very badly indeed."

And that was that. The next minute she was making him a cup of tea and describing a snow leopard documentary she and Anna had seen on TV.

Dorothea's appraisal of Agnes was a revelation. She was so definitive and matter-of-fact that Justin felt the terrible shame inside him begin to dissipate. Agnes's power was flawed, so flawed that an eleven-year-old could defy it.

Peter came into the kitchen. "Have you seen the paper today?"

Later that day Justin thought back on their conversation and wondered whether the things that killed you were not only the crashes and explosions from without, but the bombs buried deep inside, the bombs ticking quietly in your bowel or your liver or your heart, year after year, that you yourself had swallowed, or absorbed, and allowed to grow.

45

A FEW DAYS AFTER the opening, Agnes telephoned.

"I'm sorry I haven't been in touch."

Justin said nothing.

"What with the funeral and the inquest. And everything."

There was a long silence.

"Justin?"

"Yes."

"You just don't give a damn about anyone but yourself, do you?"

"You think *I* should be weeping over Ivan?"

"A man died, Justin. It's a great loss."

"A great loss? To whom? To you, maybe. To you and your career. You've lost your precious two-faced mentor."

"It wouldn't hurt to show a little remorse. After all—"

"After all what? I killed him? Tell me, what kind of genius jumps in front of a car to rescue a *coat*?"

"Justin—"

"But while we're on the subject of remorse, let's talk about *you*."

Agnes inhaled sharply. "Justin, look, I *am* sorry. I should have warned you. I should have asked you about using the pictures." She hesitated. "It was stupid of me."

"But you had more important things to think about."

"Well, as a matter of fact, I did, but it's not that. It's just that I didn't want you to get the wrong idea."

"And what would that have been?"

Agnes hesitated. "That I was using you."

"Oops! Too late."

"Justin." Her voice shook. "Don't be like that."

"OK, I won't be like that. Let's simplify things. You tell me exactly how to be and I'll be *like that*."

She said nothing.

"Oh dear," he said, "don't tell me I've hurt your feelings."

"Justin. I'm sorry I hurt you."

"IT'S-NOT-THAT-EASY." He was furious, menacing.

"I can't talk to you when you're like this."

"Do you think I *care* whether you talk to me or not?"

"But I still care about you. I want to know what you're doing, how you're feeling."

"How do you *think* I'm feeling?"

"A little angry, at a guess."

"How perceptive."

"Stop it, Justin—"

"Don't tell me what to do."

Her voice caught. "Look, I know I behaved badly. But I wish you would stop being such a—"

"Such a what? A prat? A child? A *virgin*?"

"You make it impossible to explain."

"Do I? I'm so sorry. How rude of me. *Please* explain."

"Whenever I think for a *moment* I might be talking to someone sensible it just ends up as an *idiotic* discussion about—"

"Yes?"

"About invisible dogs and fate and things I can't even begin to cope with."

"*So don't.*" He spat the words.

There was a silence.

"Why exactly do we have to be enemies?"

"Why exactly did you think it was OK to use my unhappiness for your personal gain?"

Agnes said nothing.

"Why exactly would you have sex with someone and afterwards think it was OK to ditch them, pretend it never happened, and then use their worst nightmares to further your own reputation?" *And by the way, why don't you love me anymore?*

"I *said* I'm sorry."

"Oh well, that's just *fine*, then."

"And I didn't ditch you, and I *didn't* pretend it never happened."

"It?"

"Our little sexual encounter."

"A little encounter, was it? You've had bigger, no doubt?"

"You're behaving like a child."

"Sex with a child. Isn't that against the law?"

"Jesus Christ, Justin! Weren't you there when it happened? Wasn't it your choice too? You'd just love it all to be my fault, wouldn't you? Well, it's *not*. I'm *sorry* I had sex with you and if I could take it back *I would*. Are you happy now?"

No.

"Look." Agnes tried again. "I really don't know what you want me to do or say."

He said nothing for a long time. The silence pooled stagnant between them.

At last he spoke. "I don't know either."

Liar.

You know exactly what you want her to do and say. You want her to say she loves you to distraction, you want her to beg you for sex five or six times a day, implore you to live with her, remain true to you for the rest of her life. That's all. That's what you want her to do and say.

"We'll talk again, Justin."

He had run out of comebacks.

"Say hello to Peter for me."

He didn't reply and she put down the phone. That infuriating boy. How does he expect me to love him? He's impossible to love.

Each lay awake that night thinking miserably, bitterly of the other.

Justin fell asleep first.

46

WHEN A CREATURE BEGINS to emerge from its chrysalis there is a point at which it is neither one thing nor the other, not quite grown into a new identity nor rid of the old. Its wings are folded and sticky, its colors hidden. Whether it will emerge in shades of emerald and lapis lazuli or the color of mud is yet to be revealed.

It is that long still moment of waiting that fascinates me utterly. The suspense of waiting for beauty to unfurl.

47

FOUR SHOPPING DAYS till Christmas.

Six to his birthday.

Justin stopped off at home to deliver Charlie's Christmas present and pick up a bag of gifts from his mother: a fruitcake and iced cookies in the shape of angels packed neatly in a tin for Peter's mother, and carefully wrapped presents for Peter, Anna, Dorothea, and of course himself.

His mother fussed with directions on who was to receive what, all of which she imparted without looking directly at him. Justin felt the unasked questions flapping loudly, desperately between them like a fish in a paper bag. The saddish smile on her face jolted his recollection of a time when he had loved her with a passion that was all-consuming, a time when he couldn't be left with a babysitter, wouldn't sleep in his own crib or take a bottle from his own father.

For the briefest of instants, as he watched her holding his brother close, watched the little boy's head droop onto her shoulder and his open hand laid gently on her upper arm, Justin remembered himself small and trusting and helpless, remembered the bliss of perfect communion.

What he wouldn't give for it now, for a tenth, a hundredth of that feeling. He could see it in Charlie's face, could see how he became soft and calm in the certain knowledge that nothing bad could happen as long as he was safe in those arms.

What a lie, thought Justin sadly. Like the big Santa Claus lie, except it went on longer. "We'll take care of you," said the lie, "keep you safe from the monsters that live under the bed, the dragons in the cupboard, the ghosts, the murderers and kidnappers. We'll teach you how the world works, reveal all the secrets of life." All of them, that is, except how to know yourself, find your way, be alone, survive loss and rejection, disappointment, shame, and death.

His brother wanted to get down now. His face was aimed at the blinking lights on the tree, his arms waved. He toddled over and touched each tiny bulb delicately, far too young to understand about the birth of Christianity but old enough to grasp blinking lights in his fat fist and wonder at the existence of so many pretty mysteries.

Justin had come to like being born at Christmas, for all the reasons other kids hated it. With a Christmas birthday, his transitions—from child to youth, youth to adolescent—had been muffled, sucked into the hungry, garish black hole of

The Holiday Season, leaving him free to ignore the landmarks. Just another Christmas, nothing more life-altering or life-threatening than that.

He wondered if sixteen would feel different in the way not being a virgin felt different. He wondered if he'd feel jaded in the same way, lose the fear and the excitement all at once. Once upon a time he had looked on sixteen as the gateway to adulthood. At sixteen, everything would become clear.

How could he have been so mistaken? Sixteen would change nothing, unless he got run over by a train on the day.

He looked over at his brother, who was batting a pink star with one hand, the expression on his face joyous. If you were eighteen months old and lucky, the world was one big shiny gift of needs fulfilled and fears allayed. Charlie toddled over and put his arms out for a kiss, burbling with the pleasure of it all: the stars, the kiss, the ability to initiate action. These things were enough to inspire happiness.

Releasing the child, Justin fetched the large, slightly crumpled parcel he'd hidden under the stairs and stuffed it behind the tree where it would go unnoticed until Christmas morning. Then he swept up the gifts from his mother and slipped silently out the back door.

48

THAT NIGHT, after everyone was in bed, Justin paced. Midnight. One. Two. The longest night of the year stretched ahead, dark and filled with ghosts.

He crept downstairs to find Alice. Boy padded silently after him. Opening the back door, Justin stepped outside and peered into the hutch. Alice was asleep in a mound of straw, but he shifted and raised his ears at Justin's approach.

The night was cold, the moon a few days short of full. Justin opened the little door, reached in, and heaved the great beast out, clutching him against his body for warmth. He could feel the animal's heartbeat against his own.

He stood waiting for a voice to creep out from behind a hedge, drift down a drainpipe, emerge from Alice's mouth. But there was nothing, only the outlines of the cats on the wall behind the house, silent tonight, on the prowl. For a moment at least, all was calm.

He stroked Alice, and the rabbit seemed content to slump quietly in his arms, offering the comforting heat of his great body. Boy leaned on Justin's left leg, and with a gentle sigh, dropped to the ground chest first, then rolled over sleepily onto Justin's foot and lay there, eyes half shut.

If I were a rabbit, Justin thought, I could stroll quietly through the world, minding my own business, eating bits of vegetation and snoozing. There would be no introspection, no mad flights of fancy. There would still be sex, but I'd be a bunny. It would be expected of me.

He laughed.

Gazing mesmerized into Alice's glossy upturned eye, he thought of the butcher's rabbit, half skinned, naked, singing its gruesome song.

When he looked up again, the world seemed to have shifted. The semidark of the suburban back garden appeared grainy, almost monochrome. His vision felt odd, huge and all-encompassing. The garden appeared brighter. He could see all around him without turning his head.

It felt exhilarating to experience the sky and the ground at once.

I'm a rabbit, he thought with amazement. Huge eyes, 360-degree peripheral vision, low-resolution color perception. I'm definitely a rabbit! I wonder how that happened?

Looking straight ahead, he scanned the ground and the sky at once. A bird of prey hovered far above next door's garden.

He felt frightened. What if it saw him? And those huge feral cats. He was bigger, but they would hurt him if they could. They made his skin crawl. He smelled dog. *Where?* Oh my god, *Boy*. Would Boy mistake him for a real rabbit and attack him, tear him to shreds? He looked for the dog lying at his feet, but there was no sign of him.

Wait, what was that, there, hardly moving, by the pond?

Oh god, he thought, it's a fox. A *fox*! His heart began to hammer. Dorothea's vixen! *RUN. Oh god, Alice, run run as fast as you can!*

The vixen slid closer through the underbrush, tail twitching.

She smells me! She knows I'm here. Where's Boy? Boy? Here, boy! Oh god, RUN!

In his arms, the panicky rabbit began to kick and scrabble.

She'll catch us! She's hungry. Look at her move. Look at her *eyes*! She's watching us.

Alice struggled free. Despite his huge bulk he was quick, but the fox was quicker. It made a lightning-fast lunge for the rabbit, grabbing him by the loose skin around his neck. At first Alice went limp with terror, but he came back to life and struggled furiously. Justin tried to get around the rabbit and kick the vixen away but she swung left and right opposite him, dragging the rabbit with her. In desperation, he grabbed Alice's back leg and tugged, using his other arm to grip the rabbit around the middle. Alice squeaked pitifully.

Justin looked over and saw Boy standing quietly, watching from the doorway. For a second, his eyes met the dignified eyes of his dog.

"Help!" Justin pleaded. "Help me, Boy, help us! You're a dog, for Christ's sake, we're just rabbits!"

And then something stopped him. A question. A possibility.

I am not a rabbit, he thought. *I am not.* He turned slowly away from his dog, and fixed the fox with his gaze.

I am the alpha beast, Justin said, his eyes strangely bright. Beware of *me*.

The fox went still.

The two of them stood locked in silent battle. Justin's eyes blazed with all the unexpressed fury of his life. He opened his mouth and what emerged was a snarl. Low at first, then rising in volume and intensity.

The vixen turned her head and backed away, loosening her grip on the rabbit. Justin tugged hard, and he and Alice fell backwards onto the paving stones.

He sat up. Alice squirmed in his arms. There was no sign of the fox.

"The world is full of predators," Justin murmured softly, holding the rabbit and stroking him till he lay still. "And prey."

Boy approached. His tail moved slightly back and forth. Justin freed one arm and placed it around his dog's neck.

And the lion shall lie down with the lamb, he thought, as Boy leaned his long smooth head over to meet Alice's twitching nose. Neither of them flinched.

They sat like that for a long time.

Eventually Justin replaced the rabbit in his hutch, locked the back door, and, with his dog padding silently behind him, returned to his room.

Outside the vixen shivered, her eyes dull, ribs sharply visible through her ragged coat. By the light of the moon you could see that she was starving.

Justin slipped into bed across the room from Peter, who didn't stir.

49

MY BRAVE little rabbit!

Let me remember you exactly as you are tonight.

Alive.

50

JUSTIN AWOKE the next morning with a headache.

He took a couple of painkillers.

It'll go, he thought, it's probably just the weather.

The weather was, in fact, humid and heavy; the air had the unpleasantly charged feeling that only a thunderstorm will clear.

By the time he managed to struggle through math, geography, and English, the pain at the base of his skull had set up branch offices in his temples, at the top of his head, and behind his eyeballs. He experimented with the pain, turning his head left and right, testing his fingers against each throbbing pulse, seeking remedy in pressure, position, movement.

By lunchtime he was in too much pain to consider eating and he carried himself stiffly so as not to cause unnecessary movement in his neck and shoulders.

He had cross-country after school, his last practice before they broke up for Christmas. He made his way to the track in a trance of habit. Boy brushed against his legs as he walked, and he leaned a hand on the dog's back to steady himself.

Peter smiled with pleasure at his arrival, and Justin nodded, causing a jolt so intense he had to grasp the wooden edge of the grandstand to keep from falling over. He concentrated on distributing the weight of his body evenly across both feet, clenching his teeth and groaning slightly with exertion.

Migraine, he thought. This must be what it's like to have a migraine. He could smell the fetid black blood, sticky and foul, pooling in ugly wells under his skin. The light hurt his eyes. When he squeezed them shut, tears oozed from beneath his eyelids: murky, dark, corrupt. He wondered if he could find a doctor to punch holes in his skull, insert a shunt to suck out the corrupt beings breeding within (jagged black bats, winged griffins with screeching voices). They fed on his brain, thrusting greedy mouths into the sweet yellow jelly.

"CASE! ARE YOU DEAF AS WELL AS THICK?" Coach had apparently been attempting to summon him for some time.

Justin dredged up the impulse to walk over to the track. He generally didn't mind pain; it tended to disappear if you kept running, or at least you forgot about it amid the thousand other, more familiar, pains. Perhaps this would go away too. Perhaps he could fly off the blocks, swoop through the air like a kestrel and leave it behind. From the corner of his eye (the use of peripheral vision caused a slim stiletto of icy steel to twist behind his eyeball) he thought he saw Peter looking at him oddly.

He heard Boy howl, a horrible high-pitched noise that made his teeth chatter with fear.

He crouched down, ducked his head, and from the explosion at the base of his skull, assumed he'd been struck by lightning. He sank to his knees under the force of it, toppled over on one side, teeth locked, limbs twitching with the effort of remaining alive. He looked down to see that his stomach had been ripped out of his abdomen by a gigantic vicious claw which even now was squeezing the bleeding, displaced organ till the bile gushed out of Justin's mouth.

You bastard, he thought. You bloody bastard.

Even Coach hesitated.

"That's one hell of a hangover you've got, Case." He sounded uncharacteristically nervous. "Prince, get over there and help him up. Then fill me in on the tragic details, bring a few tears to my eyes."

But Peter was already there.

The rest of the team looked on in shocked silence as Peter crouched next to his violently shuddering friend. Peter covered him with his jacket, wiped the vomit from his mouth, glanced up at the faces leaning in all around him, and spoke softly, with uncharacteristic force.

"Somebody phone an ambulance," he said very clearly so there could be no mistaking his words or their meaning. "And tell them to hurry."

51

IT IS THOUGHT that up to twenty-five percent of young adults carry the bacteria responsible for meningococcal meningitis without showing any symptoms of the disease. Of this twenty-five percent, fewer than three in 100,000 will actually go on to develop a full-fledged inflammation of the meninges, the soft membrane surrounding the brain. Direct exchange of bodily fluids with a full-blown infectious case is the surest way to guarantee infection.

You have to be fairly unlucky to contract it.

The earliest signs are common enough to make diagnosis difficult. The symptoms (fever, headache, and nausea, occasionally accompanied by a stiff neck) can easily be mistaken for cold or flu. Within anything from a few hours to a few days, however, infection of the spinal cord and the fluid surrounding the brain begins to present a new set of symptoms.

By this time, there is sometimes a rash on the palms of the hands, soles of the feet, or chest that does not fade when pressed. Extreme sensitivity to light may occur. Mental disorientation, vomiting, and high fever begin to indicate that the process of septicemia, or systemic blood poisoning, has begun.

Unfortunately, by the time any moderately observant fool can recognize these symptoms, time for the patient has begun to run out.

Justin presented unmistakably classic symptoms of bacterial meningitis to the paramedics who arrived within ten minutes of his collapse, which meant he was in imminent danger of brain damage and death. Without moving him, they inserted a needle into the cephalic vein of his right arm, attached a drip of ampicillin and chloramphenicol, and prepared to transport him to the hospital.

The medics took one look at the vomit on Peter's hands and clothes, and took him along to the hospital for treatment. They left Coach with strict instructions to compile a list of boys at the practice and present it to the health investigator who would contact him within the hour.

Having phoned ahead to Accident & Emergency with a report on Justin's condition, the medics lifted the unconscious boy and his drip onto a collapsible stretcher, transferred the stretcher to the back of the ambulance, shut the doors, activated the siren, and set off.

The entire incident, from the moment of Justin's collapse

to the instant the ambulance disappeared from sight, took less than twenty minutes.

Justin's teammates stood staring at the corner around which the ambulance had disappeared. If a flying saucer had landed on the track, taken one of them prisoner and flown off into outer space, they could not have felt more shocked. Even Coach was speechless.

At the hospital, Peter telephoned his mother, who phoned Justin's parents. Within half an hour, they had all gathered at A&E.

Back at the field, the subdued boys drifted off in ones and twos.

For a longer time than was strictly necessary, Coach remained where he was, staring transfixed at the place on the ground where Justin had fallen.

Christ, he thought. My one big chance for next year's county championship and the kid drops dead.

That bastard fate has one hell of a sense of humor.

52

IN A DARKENED ROOM, lying perfectly still on starched white sheets, his feverish body covered with a woven cotton hospital blanket, a drip attached to each arm, Justin lay in quarantine, without the strength or the desire to move.

His parents were the only visitors allowed. Gowned and masked, they took turns sitting by his bedside in silence, reading books or newspapers, occasionally looking up when he stirred, greeting the silent nurses and aides who came every quarter hour to check his blood pressure and temperature, conversing in whispers with the doctors, receiving explanations and cautious reassurances with grateful, hopeful expressions.

Justin floated in a genial amniotic bath of drugs, low light, and mental disorientation. A catheter drained waste from his bladder. He felt no pain, no interest in getting up, no hunger, no thirst, no physical desire of any kind. He had no way of knowing what day it was, what the weather might be, the names of his nurses, where he was, what was wrong with him, whether he would get better or not. Nor did he care. It was dark, it was quiet, and he was willing to float comfortably in limbo forever and ever amen.

He hated it when they asked him to do things. Squeeze my finger, a voice commanded. Wiggle your toes. Do you know your name? David, it's your mother. Can you hear me, darling? That's it, good boy, we're just going to roll you over so we can . . . Has he opened his eyes? David, can you open your eyes? It says here his name is Justin. Does he prefer one name to the other? Justin? Can you hear me, Justin? Can you lift your right hand, Justin? Just a finger? Can you blink your eyes for me, David, when you hear my voice? Can you try again?

Please stop making me try to do things. If you'd just stop making me do things I could be happy. I don't want to get better. I don't want to get worse, either, I just want to stay like this, floating gently in suspended animation, in the dark, in the pleasant, safe, silent dark.

Never mind. He's in there.

I'm in here, all right, Justin thought. I'm in here and I want to stay in here. So bugger off and let me stay in here. Let me stay for months. Let me stay forever. Let me rest in this place forever.

And sometimes, as he drifted in and out of himself, he

thought, I wonder if I'll survive. I wonder if it's necessary for me to survive. I wonder if I could simply die and have this feeling of bliss go on into infinity.

And it was with that thought, just there, that he heard the voice.

Ignore them, Justin Case. Feel how nice it is to drift? Let your body drop away. Let go, Justin Case, let it go.

Justin swooned with relief to hear the voice. It was authoritative yet kind, deep and soothing. The sound of it made him sleepy, made him feel like a child again, safe in his mother's arms. It lifted him gently and set him down in a warm buoyant sea, turquoise and calm, where he had no responsibility other than to float.

Sleep, Justin Case, I'll think for you.

The other voices, the ones he hated, interrupted with requests. Do this, squeeze that, can you sit up/open your eyes/wiggle your toes?

Never mind them, you're mine now. Sink into my arms. Let yourself be happy. See how gently I rock you to sleep? There, there, Justin Case. Let go.

There seemed to be more commotion than usual around him now. He heard the soft padding of nurses' feet, an announcement calling his parents. A man crouched over him, asking him to respond, hectoring him, shouting his name. With all the strength he had left, he shook his head, shook them off.

Go away! he wanted to shout. *Leave me alone!* He couldn't speak, but the effort produced a gurgling noise. He wanted to shield his face with one hand but found he'd forgotten how to command his limbs. For a moment there was silence. Then the smooth hands of nurses again, a prick in one arm, and for a long while nothing at all except the soft, soft dark, and the blissful silence he craved.

The next time he noticed anything, there was no voice and the wonderful soothing glow was gone. He hurt all over and his heart seemed to be beating too fast. He started to cry, silently, salt tears dripping in a steady stream from the corners of his eyes.

Don't cry, sweet boy, I'm here.

53

DURING THE TIME Justin was nonresponsive (no one at the hospital actually used the word "coma"), he was rarely alone. His parents took turns sitting with him, and when they left, one of the nurses attended him in his quarantine. Peter had been treated and released; Dorothea and Anna came with him to the hospital but were not allowed in Justin's room for fear of contagion. The girls hung pictures of Alice in the nurses' station and glued get-well cards to the smoky glass window of his room. Anna's cards, scribbled in furious frustration, read GET WELL NOW, in big black slashed letters.

Dorothea knew how she felt.

Today Dorothea had brought a painting: Justin with Boy and Alice. Her picture showed him sprawled in space with silver stars pasted over a black halo of sky. In the grass to his right was Boy, in profile, beautifully rendered in light and dark grays; the soft, dark wisdom of his eye captured exactly. To the left was Alice, drawn nearly as big as the dog. Dorothea had managed to convey a feeling for the sleepy body and the large impassive eye peering out of his white fur.

It was an extraordinary portrait of three friends.

Anna and Dorothea covered as much of the glass window as they could reach with their cards. Neither of them liked looking in at Justin lying inert, stuck full of a terrifying array of needles and tubes.

"That's not him," Anna insisted.

Dorothea agreed. The motionless body was far too quiet, devoid of Justin's nervous energy. She wondered if an unconscious person could feel anxious.

Justin's parents alternated attendance at his bedside while Charlie waited outside. His mother stayed as long as her younger child would let her. She looked terrible.

"I've neglected him," she said over and over to Peter, her face a picture of anguish. "I didn't know what to do for him."

Throughout this admission, Charlie tugged insistently at her sleeve.

I'd like to see my brother, he said. I'd like to tell him my side of the story, the side he used to know but has forgotten. I'd like to tell him to forget the big scary issues and concentrate on the ones he can control, like what he gets to eat, and whether to look at a book. Life is easier if you break it down into little segments, little desires and needs you can satisfy right now.

"Want milk!" he said aloud.

His mother dug through her bag for his milk, and the child took it, smiling at Peter.

Do you understand?

Peter nodded.

After some hesitation, he had phoned Agnes, and later that evening she came to the hospital.

"How is he?" she asked one of the night nurses, and the woman shook her head.

"Your friend do not want to wake up, honey. I never seen such a stubborn boy for staying asleep. He sleep and he sleep, and just when everybody start to think he might be getting well, he go right back to sleeping. I'm thinking he don't want to wake up."

Well, that would be about right, Agnes thought, then stopped herself guiltily.

Maybe it had nothing to do with will. Maybe he couldn't wake up even if he wanted to. She tapped softly on the window of Justin's room. His mother had gone home and it was his father who sat reading the evening paper by the light of a miniature torch, peering at a story about a London fashion designer, run over by a car and killed in a Luton rainstorm as he tried to rescue a goat. Justin's father looked up at Agnes with a tired half-smile and waved. Agnes waved back, thinking how funny the man looked peering at the small pool of illuminated type, able to make out just a few words at a time. Was he actually reading the paper, or just passing the time?

He didn't touch his son, she noticed that. When Justin's

mother was here, she sat gripping his hand, whispering apologies and promises, exhorting him to acknowledge her presence, his own presence. Please, David. Please wake up.

The more Agnes observed Justin, the more she felt certain that the nurse was right. It was easier where he was. She sighed. Poor Justin. Unable to grasp the basic notion that these people were his fate. All of them: Peter and Dorothea and Anna, his parents and brother, the doctors and nurses. Even Coach and the team and his teachers and classmates. He couldn't escape them any more than he could escape himself. Unless he decided not to wake up. Then fate would have the last laugh after all.

"Justin?" She leant in close to the window and whispered. "Don't screw up."

It's not like she's in love with you or anything, she told you that.

Shut up.

I'm right, though, am I not? She made it perfectly clear.

Shut. Up.

Let's face facts, Justin, how long do you think it will take them to get over you when you're gone?

What do you mean *when*?

I'm sorry?

You said "when you're gone."

But surely you realize it's only a matter of time? You're nearly finished, Justin Case.

Something like revulsion rose in him to hear the voice talk with such calm certainty about his death. His eyes flicked open, but his father had fallen asleep, and Agnes had turned away from the window.

He closed them again.

54

THEY DECIDED to transfer him to London.

Luton Hospital made the decision, not wishing to be the holder of the hot potato when the music stopped. No hospital wanted headlines announcing that a teenager had died of meningitis in their care. In addition, they had no idea what to do with him while he lived.

Justin's particular strain of infection had been identified and treated; he was now allowed visitors. All the medical indications pointed to the fact that he should have woken up hours, if not days, before. His brain activity seemed fine. The doctors argued over the case at staff meetings. Perhaps they had missed something, but a battery of tests revealed nothing. It seemed prudent to send him on to London and let them puzzle it out. Let him die on their watch.

As if from the bottom of a deep dark well, Justin felt himself being picked up and transferred to the ambulance. He enjoyed the slight rocking of the vehicle, the slow progress along the motorway. As they approached London he could feel the city embrace him in its humming intensity. The joyous clamor of it pelted the ambulance like hail.

At the hospital there were other noises: voices whispering nearby, sober voices in other rooms, on telephones, the clanking of trolleys, the ringing of bells—all muffled and refined into something neutral and reassuring, a gentle background bubbling as pleasant as the sound of water over stones.

Only occasionally did the voices disturb him. His mother was the worst, always pushing him to respond. It seemed to mean so much to her. Why couldn't she just leave him alone? Couldn't she see how happy he was? He didn't want to come out and play.

Justin.

The voice again. It hurt his head to listen, and he lapsed back into the warm drift of the turquoise sea.

Justin?

Go away.

You seem a bit perkier today. You might want to consider

a special offer. One day only: Clouds, pearly gates, vestal virgins, soft music, eternal happiness.

LA-LA-LALALA. I'm not listening.

You don't fool me. I can hear you think.

Who are you?

That's better.

I asked a question.

You know who I am. I'm the source of all your misery and all your delight, your choreographer, your master of ceremonies. I've waltzed you in and out of danger, and now, due to pressures on my schedule, I'm afraid it's time to finish the job.

I don't want to be finished and I'm not a job.

What's wrong with a little closure? You might enjoy getting to the end.

By "the end," I presume you mean dead?

Aren't you curious?

No.

Perhaps you're enjoying yourself too much as you are?

I've been in worse places.

You certainly have.

And whose fault is that?

Now, there's an interesting question. Whose fault, indeed?

Let me guess.

I do broad strokes, Justin. The detail is your department.

Broad strokes, how? Like crashing a DC-10 onto a sixpence where I'm supposed to be standing?

Exactly. You extricated yourself admirably, I thought.

Oh, did I? An admirable gibbering wreck, am I?

You're breaking my heart. What about all the nice things I've done for you?

Like?

Like Peter and Dorothea. Where would you be without them?

You did that for me, did you?

In a manner of speaking. Let's just say certain relationships would not have occurred had you not been in this predicament.

Great trade-off. How can I ever thank you?

What about Agnes?

What about her?

She did quite nicely with your rites of passage.

Nicely for whom? It was a disaster.

I see. So, the good things are all your own devise, the bad all mine?

Sounds about right.

I don't think you understand me at all.

Ditto. I'm going to sleep.

You are asleep. But before you go, I require your signature on this simple form. There is absolutely no risk, you pay nothing up front, and if you are not totally satisfied—

Yes, what if I'm not?

Ah, but you will be.
Justin?
Justin?
Pleasant dreams.

55

ON CHRISTMAS EVE, Justin was settled into a busy ward. It was hoped that the increased activity might encourage his return to consciousness. Peter and Dorothea arrived at midafternoon on the train and walked the ten minutes from station to hospital through the dirty gray streets. All around them people bustled with last-minute shopping, bad-tempered and resentful at the exigencies of the giving season.

At the hospital, Peter's talent for invisibility proved more useful than ever. He had a way of slipping in quietly to sit with his friend when everyone else had gone home, or gone to lunch, or simply become bored and wandered off. Sometimes he brought a book. Other times he just stared into space thinking, or talked quietly to Justin, or to himself.

He wondered about Boy, searched for him every night when he went home. Dorothea hadn't seen him either.

"Your dog's missing again, Justin. I don't want you to worry, that's not why I'm telling you. It's just that I get the feeling he needs you to exist. Needs you conscious, that is."

Peter paused.

"I wish you could see Dorothea's portrait of you. She's drawn you and Boy and Alice like some kind of secular Holy Family. It's a very beautiful picture."

And then later, he whispered to his friend.

"Try to remember what I said about bad science, Justin. Try to be careful, please."

Dorothea arrived, bearing two cups of tea from the ward's galley kitchen. She handed one to Peter and sat down, her face dark with frustration. "He doesn't look any different," she said.

Peter nodded. "Maybe he's thinking it all through."

"All *what?*"

Peter smiled wanly. "Who knows? Life and death, probably. Himself."

"This is no place to think. If he hangs around too long looking like that they'll cart him off to the morgue. And it'll serve him right, too."

Peter looked at his sister, at the stormy eyes and the querulous curve of her mouth. "I know," he said.

He rose to his feet and left her with Justin while he went outside to phone his mother.

Dorothea sat gingerly on the edge of the chair beside Justin's bed. She didn't like to look at him. She didn't like seeing him this way, his face drained of color, his mouth slack. She tried to marshal the proper feelings of sympathy and compassion, but the longer she sat, the more angry she felt.

"Justin?" She poked his shoulder, not gently. "Stop thinking about yourself for a change. The answer isn't in your head, it's out here, with us."

Dorothea?

She paused.

Dorothea?

"What am I supposed to do? I won't sit by your bed being all lovey-dovey trying to convince you not to be dead. It's cheap, and it's cowardly. And you're better than that, at least I thought you were."

Please don't go.

"You're not even thinking about the rest of us, how we might feel. We need you to be alive, your dog needs you to be alive. You've got a brother. Your family's distraught and it's all your fault." Dorothea glowered, as a doctor with his band of residents arrived for ward rounds.

She stood up to go, then leant in close, fuming. "If you want to be dead so much, then bloody well *be* dead," she hissed. "But don't expect me to cry at your funeral."

She turned and stalked off.

56

JUSTIN'S FAMILY celebrated Christmas morning in a hotel room near the hospital. It was a short celebration involving a hastily purchased plastic tree and a box full of gifts transported from Luton. Charlie unwrapped each present with careful deliberation, saving the large lumpy one with reindeer wrapping for last.

The hospital canteen featured a festive menu of turkey or ham, cranberry or bread sauce, sprouts or peas, chestnut or sage stuffing, and Christmas pudding with brandy butter or cream. Pushing trays around the low-ceilinged, tinsel-strung room were a mix of relatives and patients, junior staff, nurses, cleaners, and doctors without sufficient seniority to invoke holiday leave.

Charlie attracted a disproportionate amount of attention from the adults present in part because he was the only child in the canteen, and in part because of the oversized stuffed dog clamped firmly under one arm. His parents let him cruise from table to table, secure in the knowledge that eventually someone would send him back in their direction. He took advantage of his freedom, accepting kind words and treats from around the room, then setting off to explore the kitchens, the loos, the supply cupboards, and finally the wards. There he graciously accepted chocolates from bored patients and other children's grandparents, many of whom were happy to celebrate Christmas by feeding him sweets and engaging in predominantly one-sided conversations.

When he had eaten his fill, the little boy tottered off down the hall to find his brother. He hadn't been allowed to see him alone, but today he was determined. He wanted to thank him for his beautiful greyhound, and had something important to say to him as well.

It took some time to orientate himself in the maze of wards, but at last he found a familiar landmark, and another, and another. He launched himself rapidly along, lurching side to side as he ran.

He found his brother's unresponsive figure at last, and though he was too young to understand about meningitis and comas, he had his own ideas of what was going on.

"He's just sleeping," his mother had said, "gone bye-byes."

But the child thought, *Nobody sleeps through Christmas*.

The little boy stood staring for a long moment, then pressed his sticky mouth up against Justin's face. He stood that way for some time, breathing his soft child's breath into his brother's ear, and breathing, too, the thoughts he'd been forming slowly and carefully over the past week.

I like being in London, he whispered, I like the big red buses and the bouncy bed in the hotel and the big window I can look out, but I don't like the hospital because everyone here seems sick or sad and most of all I don't like you lying here looking dead.

Justin's foot twitched.

I'm sorry I started all this by trying to fly and I'd take it back if I could but I can't, so please think of it from my point of view: if you die I will have a dead brother and it will be me instead of you who suffers.

Justin thought of his brother on that warm summer day, standing up on the windowsill holding both their futures, light and changeable as air, in his outstretched arms.

Of course, Justin thought, I'm part of his fate just as he's part of mine. I hadn't considered it from his point of view. Or from the point of view of the universe, either. It's just a playing field crammed full of cause and effect, billions of dominoes, each knocking over billions more, setting off trillions of actions every second. A butterfly flaps its wings in Africa and my brother in Luton thinks he can fly.

The child nodded. A piano might fall on your head, he said, but it also might not. And in the meantime you never know. Something nice might happen.

He put his warm hand on his brother's cool, motionless one. I'm going now, said Charlie, they'll be looking for me soon. But I'll leave you my dog for company.

He's your dog.

I know he is, but you can have him for now.

"See you later," murmured the child, pressing his lips to his brother's ear before setting off.

"OK," Justin replied, weakly but distinctly. And then with a good deal of effort, he opened his eyes to meet the deep black ones of his brother's Christmas dog, soft wise eyes that blinked slowly back at him.

57

I FEEL A LITTLE SAD, now it's over, I enjoyed our game. It hardly ever fails.

Except, of course, when it does.

And that can be interesting too.

58

SO WHAT HAPPENED in the end?

This much we know: Justin and Agnes lived happily ever after. And sadly ever after. Sometimes at the same time. And not necessarily with each other. Till the very end of time.

Whenever that was.

In the meantime, Charlie learned to fly. Dorothea fell in love. Peter discovered a new star. And a great number of things happened to Justin. Hundreds of millions of ordinary, unexpected, and occasionally quite astonishing things.

And that was his fate.

59

THE VIEW IS FINE *from here. I can look down across the world and see everything.*

For instance, I can see you.

ABOUT THE AUTHOR

Meg Rosoff was born in Boston and had three or four careers in publishing and advertising before starting to write. In 1989 she moved from New York City to London, where she lives with her husband and their daughter. Her phenomenal first novel, *How I Live Now*, won several awards in the United States and Europe, among them the Michael L. Printz Award, the *Guardian* Award for Children's Fiction, the Branford Boase Award, and the Luchs Prize, awarded by *Die Zeit* and Radio Bremen in Germany.